The magic wishbone

"Should anything go amiss," said Magister Stephanus, *"should you be in distress or danger, break it in two. It will take you wherever you wish to be."*

"Is that all it can do?" asked Lionel.

"Since it might save your life," Stephanus replied curtly, *"I should consider that quite sufficient. You need only wish yourself home, snap the bone, and home you shall be in an instant."*

"Now I understand," said Lionel. *"With that, there's nothing that can harm me."*

"I wouldn't be quite so sure of that," said Stephanus. *"In Brightford, you'll find beasts crueler than any roaming Dunstan Forest."* He tucked the wishbone into a small pouch of soft leather which he closed with a drawstring and hung around Lionel's neck.

"[An] exuberant, tongue-in-cheek commentary on human foibles." —*Booklist*

"A comic and ebullient fantasy, just right for reading aloud." —*The Horn Book*

"The style, the humor, the play on words, the rumbustious characters, and the pace of the action are delightful." —*The Bulletin of the Center for Children's Books*

The Cat Who
Wished to Be a Man

BOOKS BY LLOYD ALEXANDER

The Prydain Chronicles
The Book of Three
The Black Cauldron
The Castle of Llyr
Taran Wanderer
The High King
The Foundling

The Westmark Trilogy
Westmark
The Kestrel
The Beggar Queen

The Vesper Holly Adventures
The Illyrian Adventure
The El Dorado Adventure
The Drackenberg Adventure
The Jedera Adventure
The Philadelphia Adventure

Other Books for Young People
The Arkadians
The Cat Who Wished to Be a Man
The First Two Lives of Lukas-Kasha
Gypsy Rizka
The Iron Ring
The Marvelous Misadventures of Sebastian
The Remarkable Journey of Prince Jen
Time Cat
The Town Cats and Other Tales
The Wizard in the Tree

The Cat Who
Wished to Be a Man

LLOYD ALEXANDER

PUFFIN BOOKS

PUFFIN BOOKS

Published by the Penguin Group

Penguin Putnam Books for Young Readers,

345 Hudson Street, New York, New York 10014, U.S.A.

Penguin Books Ltd, 27 Wrights Lane, London W8 5TZ, England

Penguin Books Australia Ltd, Ringwood, Victoria, Australia

Penguin Books Canada Ltd, 10 Alcorn Avenue, Toronto, Ontario, Canada M4V 3B2

Penguin Books (N.Z.) Ltd, 182-190 Wairau Road, Auckland 10, New Zealand

Penguin Books Ltd, Registered Offices: Harmondsworth, Middlesex, England

First published in the United States of America by E. P. Dutton & Co., Inc., 1973
Published by Puffin Books,
a member of Penguin Putnam Books for Young Readers, 2000

1 3 5 7 9 10 8 6 4 2

THE LIBRARY OF CONGRESS HAS CATALOGED THE E. P. DUTTON EDITION AS FOLLOWS:

Alexander, Lloyd. The cat who wished to be a man.
Summary: When he begins dealing with humanity, Lionel the cat begins to
understand why his wizard master was reluctant to change him into a man.
[1. Magic—Fiction.] I. Title.
PZ7.A3774Cat [Fic] 73-77447
ISBN 0-525-27545-2

Puffin Books ISBN 0-14-130704-8

Printed in the United States of America

Reprinted by arrangement with Penguin Putnam Books for Young Readers.

For us, born human,
to make the best of it.

~§ CONTENTS §~

Contents

The Cat Who
Wished to Be a Man

CHAPTER I

In Which Lionel Begs a Favor

❧ "Please, master," said the cat, "will you change me into a man?"

At the fireplace, Magister Stephanus was stirring the soup kettle. A high wizard, Stephanus could have commanded the soup to look after itself; but he preferred to do his own cooking. He stopped short and frowned at the young orange-tawny cat.

"What's that you say? Lionel, did I hear you correctly?"

"Master, will you change me into a man?"

"I gave you the power of speech so that we might talk intelligently together," Stephanus replied. "But if you're going to talk nonsense, I shall take it away. Man, indeed! You're not even a full-grown cat."

"But, master—" said Lionel, "I don't feel like a cat."

"You are not old enough to know how you feel about anything at all," said Stephanus. "Furthermore, would you kindly tell me: Since when does a cat not feel like a cat?"

"Since you gave me human speech."

Stephanus jumped to his feet, sending Lionel scurrying behind the milk jugs. The wizard's homespun robe flapped around his shins as he paced the earthen floor of the cottage, tugging his beard and groaning:

"Unbearable! Intolerable! Another gift ill-used! I give the power of speech to a cat; the magnificent treasure of language—and he torments me with it!"

Lionel poked his head around a milk jug. "Please, master, I do want to be a man."

"Be glad you are a cat!" Stephanus cried. "Let me tell you about men: Wolves are gentler. Geese are wiser. Jackasses have better sense. And you—I warn you, don't try my patience."

Next morning, Lionel found Magister Stephanus working in the garden, tying up his beanstalks.

"Master," pleaded Lionel, "will you change me into a man?"

Stephanus flung down the beanpole, swallowed hard a few times, and replied:

"Listen to me. Many years before I built this cottage in Dunstan Forest, I lived in Brightford—"

"Brightford?" Lionel broke in. "What's that?"

"A town," said Stephanus. "Crammed with humans, packed in, each one jammed on top of his neighbor."

"Like a beehive? Or anthill?" said Lionel. "I'd like to see that."

The wizard snorted. "Bees don't sting so spitefully as

humans; ants work harder. When I first came there, the folk of Brightford were tilling their soil with pointed sticks. I pitied them in those days. So I gave them a gift: all the secrets of metalworking. I taught them to forge iron for plows, rakes, and hoes."

"They must have been glad for such tools."

"Tools? They made swords and spears! There's not one gift I gave them they didn't turn inside out, upside down, and wrong side to. They were a feeble, sickly lot, so I taught them to use roots and herbs for medicines. They found a way to brew deadly poisons. I taught them to make mild wine; they distilled strong brandy! I taught them to raise cows and horses as helpful friends; they turned them into drudges. Selfish creatures! They care for nothing, not even for each other. Love? They love only gold."

"What's gold?" asked the cat, more curious than ever.

"A yellow substance. Men treasure it."

"It must be delicious," Lionel said. "I wish I could taste some."

Stephanus laughed bitterly. "You can't eat it. You can't drink it. It's yellow dirt, nothing more. But those fools turned it into coins; round, flat bits of metal. Money, as they call it. By any name, worthless. But they'll do anything to get their hands on it.

"There was a man in Brightford," Stephanus went on, "who pleaded with me to build a bridge, so farmers and tradesmen could cart their wares across the river. And so I did. For the sake of all the townsfolk, I built a sturdy bridge, stone by stone. When I finished, that villain set up a toll gate."

"I know what a gate is," Lionel said, "but what's a toll?"

"It means paying out money," Stephanus answered. "An activity these creatures find either disagreeable or delightful, depending on whether they're paying or being paid. And that greedy fellow made everyone pay, coming and going across my bridge. Instead of putting a stop to his doings, the Town Council made him their leader. They voted him Mayor."

"Mayor?" asked Lionel. "What's that mean?"

"In this case, it means he got even richer. After that, I could stomach no more. I came to Dunstan Forest. Never, never will I set foot in Brightford. Nor shall you. And not another word on the matter."

The next morning, while Stephanus was kneading dough for the week's baking, Lionel jumped onto the table:

"Master, please change me into a man."

Stephanus picked up the rolling pin, set it down, and took several deep breaths. After a few moments, having calmed himself, he said:

"Let us talk reasonably, you and I. My dear Lionel, I understand your feelings perfectly. All of us, at one time or another, grow a little weary of what we are. Sometimes, I tire of being a wizard. Sometimes, you tire of being a cat. It's quite normal. Very well. You shall be—oh, let us say, a badger. For a few days. A refreshing change. Or an otter? A bird of some sort? Whatever you prefer."

"Master," said Lionel, "I do so wish to be a man, and see Brightford for myself."

"Stubborn cat!" Stephanus burst out. "I warned you!"

Lionel laid his ears flat against his head, sprang down from the table, and was about to dash away.

"Stop!" shouted Stephanus. "Stand where you are. You've tried my patience beyond bearing. Now take your punishment. Do you want to be a man and go to Brightford? Then you shall!"

"Master, you grant my favor? Thank you!"

"Save your thanks until you're cured of your folly," answered Stephanus. "Oh, indeed, you'll go to Brightford this very day. One thing, however, you must promise me."

"Gladly!" cried Lionel. "Anything!"

"You must give me your word," said Stephanus, "your solemn vow that you'll come home without delay."

"Master, I promise. I swear!"

"So be it. Let's get on, then. I've better things to do than change cats into men. Hold still."

Lionel obeyed. Now that his master had at last agreed, the cat's eagerness turned to fear. He shut his eyes tight, curled himself into a ball, with his paws hugging his chest, hind legs drawn up, and his tail wrapped around his haunches. He waited.

"Stand up," commanded Stephanus.

Lionel blinked. His front paws were hands. Openmouthed, he stared at the ten fingers and wiggled them first with caution, then delight. His hind paws were a pair of feet; his claws, a set of toes. His tail had vanished; his whiskers, too.

"Is it done?" Lionel whispered, wonder-struck. "So quickly? Is that all there is to it?"

"What did you expect?" retorted Stephanus. "Thunder and lightning?"

CHAPTER II

A Gift from Magister Stephanus

❧ "Master, thank you!"

Pouncing upon the wizard, Lionel tried to jump into his master's lap. He succeeded only in sending both himself and Stephanus sprawling to the floor.

"Off my chest, you great lummox!" fumed Stephanus. "You're not a kitten!"

Lionel helped the wizard to his feet, realizing now that he was a head taller than Stephanus. In amazement, he examined his new body, lean and well-muscled, with a trim waist and broad shoulders. He patted his long arms and legs, counted and re-counted his fingers and toes; then, eager to be on his way, he started for the cottage door.

"Come back here," Stephanus ordered. "How far do you think you'll go in Brightford as you are?"

"As I am? You've made me better than I ever hoped."

"Without a stitch!"

"Do I have to be sewn together?" asked Lionel, dismayed.

"I mean," said Stephanus, "that you are stark naked."

"Does it matter?"

Shaking his head, sighing and muttering, Stephanus opened an iron chest in the corner. He rummaged inside and finally took out a pair of boots, a shirt, breeches, a jacket, and some linen which he handed to Lionel.

"Wear these. They should fit you well enough."

Lionel eagerly pulled on the clothing. A moment later, however, he groaned:

"Master, I can't go to Brightford!"

"What are you talking about?" returned the exasperated wizard. "First, you want nothing else in the world. Now, you say you can't go."

"I'm choking to death!" Lionel gasped. "I can't breathe! I can't walk!"

"That doesn't surprise me," replied Stephanus, "since you've got your arms in the legs of your breeches, and your legs in your shirtsleeves. And your boots on the wrong feet."

"But they're the only feet I have now."

Clicking his tongue impatiently, Magister Stephanus tried to put the garments right. Since the wizard was unused to dressing anyone but himself, and Lionel unused to dressing at all, between them they only made matters worse. But Lionel, defter than his master, finally caught the knack of the buttons and buttonholes, laces and eyelets, and soon stood fully clothed.

The wizard studied his former cat with reluctant admiration, and nodded curtly:

"You'll do. No worse than the others. Here," he added,

taking a looking glass out of the chest, "you might as well see for yourself."

Lionel stared at the reflection. The nose was much longer than his old one, and his mouth wider; but his rough crop of hair was the same tawny color his fur had been; and his eyes, the same gold-flecked green. He moistened his finger ends with the tip of his tongue and began smoothing his eyebrows and scrubbing his ears.

"No need to preen yourself," said Stephanus. "It won't make any difference. Humans all look much alike. Come here, I have something important for you."

Handing back the looking glass, Lionel waited while Magister Stephanus peered into a wooden box filled with coins, rings, trinkets, and oddments.

"I don't intend to coddle you," said the wizard, stirring the jumble with a forefinger. "No magic shields or any such trappings. Should you come a-cropper in Brightford, so much the worse for you. It will be a good lesson. Nevertheless, I can't have you going among those humans without some protection. Ah, yes—this is what I was looking for."

"A wishbone?" said Lionel, sniffing at the dry, brittle object Stephanus held out to him.

"Precisely."

"Do I chew it up now?"

"The function of a wishbone," said Stephanus, "is to be wished upon. But it can be used only once."

"Master, you've already given me everything I could wish for."

"So you think at the moment. Later, your opinion

may change; which is why you must carry this with you. Should anything go amiss, should you be in distress or danger, break it in two. It will take you wherever you wish to be."

"Is that all it can do?" asked Lionel.

"Since it might save your life," Stephanus replied curtly, "I should consider that quite sufficient. You need only wish yourself home, snap the bone, and home you shall be in the instant."

"Now I understand," said Lionel. "With that, there's nothing can harm me."

"I wouldn't be quite so sure of that," said Stephanus. "In Brightford, you'll find beasts crueler than any roaming Dunstan Forest." He tucked the wishbone into a small pouch of soft leather which he closed with a drawstring and hung around Lionel's neck. "Therefore, you must keep this with you at all times."

"Thank you, master," cried Lionel, embracing the wizard, this time with more caution. "Farewell."

"And your promise—"

"I won't forget it," Lionel assured him.

"Off with you, then," said Stephanus. "Keep the sun to your back until you're through the woods. Go left and you'll come to Brightford Road. Farewell," he murmured, gently stroking Lionel's head. "Farewell, poor, foolish cat. You'll come home once you've had your fill. And that, I daresay, will be sooner than you think."

CHAPTER III

Mayor Pursewig's Toll Gate

✦ Following his master's directions, Lionel set off through Dunstan Forest. He loped along, swiftly and silently, never cracking a twig under his feet. He cocked his head at every rustling among the trees, ready to pounce at every shadow. When a plump quail scurried across his path, Lionel's eyes brightened, his nose twitched; but he kept himself from dropping to hands and knees and darting after the bird. He hurried on and by mid-morning reached the edge of the woods.

There, he scampered down a wide, hard-packed surface, which he took to be Brightford Road. Soon, rounding a turn, he cried out in wonder. Ahead rose rooftops higher than he had ever imagined. A stone bridge arched over a quick-flowing river. Folk of every size jostled their way across; some afoot, some on horseback; some driving wagons, others trundling wheelbarrows. Beyond, he glimpsed an open square. Banners waved over stands of vegetables and fruit, tubs of fish, and mounds of cheese. His nose tingled at the aroma of sausages, roasting chickens, and hot pastries.

Lionel ran to follow the crowd. However, he was only halfway across the bridge when a wooden gate bristling with spikes came rattling down in front of him. A leather-jacketed man with what looked like a cook-pot on his head seized Lionel's arm:

"You! Where do you think you're going?"

"To Brightford," Lionel answered. "But my time's short. So, if you'd be kind enough to move your fence away—"

"Pay your toll," the man snapped, "and no back talk."

"Why, this must be the toll gate," replied Lionel, "just as my master said."

"What did you think it was, you simpleton? Mayor Pursewig's horse and carriage? So dig into your pockets and let's have the money."

The man had gestured at Lionel's breeches, which Lionel found to hold pouches made of cloth. Glad to oblige, he searched through them, then shook his head. "They're empty. Magister Stephanus, didn't give me any money. I'm sorry, I can't pay anything today. But if I ever come to Brightford again—"

"Hear that?" cried the man to his comrade, who was dressed in the same kind of jacket and helmet. "He's a sharp one, eh?" He turned back to Lionel. "Come on, I've no time for games. Pay or swim."

"I'd rather not swim," said Lionel. He glanced down at the river and shuddered. "I'm not fond of water."

"Then get off the bridge," commanded the guard, picking up a curved piece of wood set in a long handle. He pointed it at Lionel, who watched him with interest:

"What's that? A plow?"

"I'll plow you with it," retorted the guard. "You'll have a bolt from my crossbow in your gizzard. Away with you!"

By this time, the crowd behind Lionel had grown larger and less patient. Some shouted angrily for him to step aside; others, for the guards to let him pass.

"Have done!" called out a burly wagoner, whose horse had begun pawing the ground. "Open the gate! Let us all go through. Free! Pursewig's made his fortune three times over with his toll bridge!"

"That's right!" cried a woman with a basket on her arm. "He's squeezed enough out of us. And so did his father! And his grandfather before him!"

"Up with the gate!" another joined in. "We pay so much toll, we've nothing left for ourselves!"

"Up with the gate!" added more voices. "Up with the gate! And down with Pursewig!"

Hearing this last, the two guards in alarm shouted for reinforcements and aimed their crossbows at the towns-folk who were pressing forward.

"Back! Back, all of you!" came the harsh voice of a man who thrust his way roughly through the crowd.

This new arrival wore a broad-brimmed hat with a white plume; at his neck, a ruffle of linen; around his waist, a wide red sash. At his side hung a blade longer than the one Magister Stephanus used for cutting weeds.

"What's afoot here?" he demanded. "What's this insolence about His Honor the Mayor?"

"Captain Swaggart—" one of the guards began.

"We've had our fill of Pursewig's toll gate," the wagoner declared. "That's not insolence, that's plain fact!"

"Hold your tongue, Tolliver," snapped Swaggart, turning his long-jawed face to the wagoner. "I might have known you had a finger in this."

"Here's the one who started it," said the guard, pointing at Lionel. "He wouldn't pay his toll."

"So that's it," said Swaggart, hooking his thumbs into his sash, and looking up and down through narrowed eyes at Lionel. "A wiseacre come to Brightford. Well, pay up or go back. That's the law for every man, woman, and child."

"In that case," Lionel said happily, "I needn't pay at all. I'm a cat."

CHAPTER IV

Lionel Crosses a Bridge

🐘 Hearing this, the townspeople forgot their anger at Mayor Pursewig's toll gate and burst into laughter. Swaggart stepped closer to Lionel and said between clenched teeth:

"Have a care. You'll do your joking in Brightford jail."

"It's true," Lionel replied. "Indeed, I'm a cat."

A mocking grin crawled over Swaggart's face. He stretched out a hand and tickled Lionel under the chin, crying in a mincing voice:

"Puss-puss-puss! Kitty-kitty-kitty!"

Lionel drew back. The rude touch made the hairs rise at his neck. His eyes blazed, his hands flew up, fingers bent, ready to scratch.

"Oho," crowed Swaggart, "Master Puss is a wildcat! Mind your manners or I'll trim your claws. Where are you from? What's your trade? Village idiot?"

"I live in Dunstan Forest with my master," Lionel answered, calmer now that Swaggart had stopped fingering him. "As to my trade, I don't have one. Aside from being a cat."

"Isn't that remarkable!" said Swaggart, circling Lionel and peering at him from every side. "A cat! Whatever became of your tail? Did the mice get it?"

"No," Lionel explained earnestly. "I don't have it with me. You see, what happened is this: Magister Stephanus changed me into a man."

"Into a jackass," corrected Swaggart.

"Stephanus thinks highly of them," said Lionel. "Perhaps I'll try being one another time. But I gave my word I'd come home without delay. So, if you don't mind opening the gate—"

"Is it in your way, Master Puss? A great cat like you can jump over it easily. Go on, Puss, let's see how well you leap. Clear the gate and you go free into Brightford. Better yet, all of you here will go in free."

"Let him be, Swaggart," called the wagoner named Tolliver. "I'll pay his toll. Jump the gate? If he doesn't break his neck, he'll skewer himself on the spikes."

Lionel, meantime, glad to make such an easy bargain, had stepped back a couple of paces. In a glance, his sharp eyes took the measure of the gate. He crouched, tensed his muscles; with a powerful spring he launched himself into the air; and went sailing over, with room to spare, to land lightly on his feet on the other side.

Behind him, the astonished guards opened the toll gate. Cheering, whistling, shouting with glee, the crowd streamed across the bridge.

While Swaggart glared after him, Lionel ran to the cobbled square. No sooner there, he clapped his hands over his ears, sure they would split from the honking, gabbling, bleating, and whinnying that rose from every side. At gaily decorated booths, the occupants hammered pots and pans, stitched pieces of leather into boots, or unrolled bolts of cloth, shouting for the townsfolk to come and buy. In one corner stood a dozen men blowing into long brass tubes or thumping what seemed to be barrels with skins tightly stretched across both ends; and all making the loudest braying, booming, and twittering that Lionel had ever heard.

"One thing sure," he thought. "Humans are a noisy sort. How can they ever sleep? Are they all deaf?"

To his surprise, however, the racket from the band shortly became more agreeable. As Lionel grew used to it, the sound quickened his pulse and set his feet tapping.

He set off to find the meats and pastries he had scented before. But he had only taken a few steps when he felt something flutter like a mouse in one of his pockets. Lionel's hand darted in and gripped it.

"Let me go! Let me go!" squealed a tight-faced man, thin as a weasel, squirming to free his wrist from Lionel's grasp.

"Were you looking for something?" Lionel asked politely.

"All right, you've hooked me!" the man burst out. "Don't call the Town Watch. We'll strike a bargain. How much to let me go?"

"How much?" repeated Lionel. "How much of what?"

The man pulled a fistful of metal disks from his pocket and forced them into Lionel's hand. "There! Now, get your paws off me!"

As Lionel, puzzled, stared at this unexpected gift, his benefactor seized the chance to break loose and take to his heels.

"Here, wait!" called Lionel. But the man had vanished into the crowd. Lionel sniffed at the handful of coins. "This must be what Stephanus called money."

He picked up one of the disks and popped it into his mouth, only to spit it out immediately. "Stephanus was right. It doesn't taste good at all."

Lionel moved on, pausing by one of the booths to wonder at a bright red cart wheel, with numbers painted around the rim, attached to an upright post.

"Step closer, friend," called a beefy, heavy-cheeked man. "Don't be shy with Master Pickerel. Dame Fortune smiles on you today! What's your pleasure? A turn of the wheel? A roll of the dice? Any small wager—" His eyes popped at the money in Lionel's hands. "Or a large one. Come, friend, put that down for double or nothing."

Unsure what this meant, but glad to oblige such a cordial fellow, Lionel did as he was asked and spread the coins over the wooden table. Seeing a newcomer about to try his luck, the onlookers gathered closer.

Lionel, meantime, had glimpsed three large walnut shells on the table. To his disappointment, they were empty.

Master Pickerel's smile widened. "So, you want a go at that, do you?"

Without waiting for Lionel's answer, he put down a dried pea, covered it with one shell and set the other two beside it.

"Look sharp," ordered Pickerel, sliding the shells back and forth, round and about with great speed and deftness. At last, he stopped and grinned at Lionel:

"Now, then. Find the pea and win your wager. Where is it? Under this one? Or this? Or this?"

Lionel's eyes had followed every motion, and he promptly answered:

"None of them. You have it yourself."

Before Pickerel realized what was happening, Lionel quickly reached out and spread open the man's fingers. Pickerel, caught unawares, stammered and sputtered. The dried pea lay in his palm, where he had hidden it from the start.

"Caught at your own game, Pickerel!" cried one of the onlookers, while the others guffawed.

"Did I win?" asked Lionel. "Try again. This time, see if you can hide it better."

"Robber! Swindler!" bellowed the furious Pickerel. However, in face of so many witnesses, he had no choice but to give Lionel double his money. "Don't come back! I'll not gamble with cheaters like you!"

CHAPTER V

Master Swaggart Deals a Hand of Cards

◊► Lionel now had so many coins he could scarcely hold them. The onlookers cheered him, nudged him in the ribs, clapped him on the back, and one cried:

"Celebrate your good luck! Let's have some food and drink!"

"Gladly," agreed Lionel, whose appetite was growing sharper every moment. He let himself be hustled along in the midst of these new companions, so good-natured and helpful that he wondered how Stephanus could think ill of them. As they halted at a booth loaded with meats and dainties of all sorts, a man wearing a head-piece like a white mushroom leaned out and demanded:

"Who'll pay for this?"

"He will," spoke up one of Lionel's comrades, pushing him to the fore. "Treats for all!"

Lionel was more than willing to hand over as many coins as the cook asked for, delighted to exchange the bits of metal for something much tastier. The cook hauled down links of sausage, whole roasted chickens, meat pies, and puddings, sailing them into the crowd as fast as he could. But Lionel, busy supplying the man with coins, had no chance to capture any of these flying victuals for himself. He was about to snatch at a pie when he heard a voice behind him:

"So, Master Puss! No money for the toll, eh? But enough to treat every idler in Brightford!"

Swaggart, glaring at him coldly, went on:

"Where did you get it? Steal it? No, you'll tell me you found it lying in the street."

"One man gave me some for unhooking him," Lionel answered. "Another, for playing a game with nutshells."

"Why, of course they did!" scoffed Swaggart. "So you just step along with me to the guardhouse and tell your tale in comfort."

"Willingly," said Lionel. "You're welcome to sausages, too, if you like. There's plenty of money left."

"Is there, now?" said Swaggart, quickly softening his tone. "You'd better have a care. There's rogues in Brightford itching to get their fingers on a man's gold. But don't worry. I'll see you're well looked after."

"Why, that's very thoughtful of you," said Lionel, pleased at such a friendly offer.

Swaggart led him from the square to a stone building and there ushered Lionel through an iron-studded doorway. No sooner was Lionel in the room than he began coughing, choking, and gasping for breath. Some dozen men, dressed like the two he had seen at the bridge, lounged in corners or sat around a wooden table. Most of them gripped long clay tubes between their teeth. Smoke billowed from the ends of these tubes and even streamed from the men's noses and mouths.

"Fire! Fire!" cried Lionel. He would have turned tail then and there, but Swaggart held him back.

"Never fear," Swaggart assured him, grinning. "My Town Watchmen have it under control. Let's get down to our own little business."

Lionel rubbed his watering eyes and glanced around uneasily, still afraid the room would go up in flames. The Town Watchmen, however, kept puffing away and even seemed to enjoy it. The men at the table had begun passing around brightly colored pieces of pasteboard which they studied with great interest.

Swaggart, meanwhile, pulled over a stool and gestured for Lionel to sit. "Now, Master Puss, I hope you're not going to tell me some cock-and-bull story."

"No, indeed," said Lionel. "It's nothing to do with livestock." Putting the remainder of his coins on the table, he explained how he had come by them.

Swaggart eyed him sharply. "Well, Puss, it may be that you're telling the truth. Though I doubt it. But watch your step. Try no tricks, do you hear? Wait, hold on there," he added as Lionel rose to leave. "What about your passport?"

"Passport?"

"You haven't got one?" said Swaggart. "Ah, my dear

friend, that won't do. You'll need one if you mean to stay in Brightford. And what about your dog license?"

"No need for that, whatever it is," said Lionel. "The less I have to do with dogs, the better."

"Exactly," Swaggart hastily replied. "A license *not* to keep a dog, Master Cat. And another license for using the streets—"

One of the Town Watchmen was seized with a violent fit of coughing. Another puffed out his cheeks and stared at the ceiling. Swaggart, meantime, had been jotting down sums on a scrap of paper:

"These fees are costly," he said. "But the law's the law, and a fine fellow like you wouldn't want to break it. But you're in luck. All told, it comes to the very penny of what you have here."

Scooping up the money, Swaggart pocketed the coins and handed Lionel some of the bright-colored pasteboards. "Here, take your licenses."

"I'm grateful to you," said Lionel, relieved that he had avoided breaking any rule. "I hate to trouble you, but I'm still hungry. If I have none of that money to trade for food, what shall I do?"

Swaggart poked his tongue first into one cheek, then the other, and gave Lionel a long, sideways look. "I do believe you're a true, natural-born mooncalf."

"No," Lionel replied, "a cat, as I told you."

"Well, now, Master Puss," returned Swaggart, "you just go up the street here, to the inn. The Crowned Swan. The finest food in Brightford. March right through the door. Find Mistress Gillian. Then tell her to bring you the best dinner in the house."

"This Mistress Gillian—she won't ask for money?"

"Not a penny," said Swaggart, pushing Lionel out the door. "All you do is take her by the waist and give her a good, round, lip-smacking kiss."

In the street, Lionel eagerly set off in the direction Swaggart pointed out. Then he stopped and frowned.

"I forgot to ask," he said to himself, "whatever is a kiss?"

CHAPTER VI

Mistress Gillian Picks Up Her Broom

§► Lionel turned back, tried the door, and found it locked. From within, he heard bursts of laughter. Though he knocked long and loud, no one came. So he stepped into the street and hurried along until he saw, over the doorway of a wood-and-plaster house, a board bearing a gold-crowned white swan that looked as if it would swim away at any moment. Lionel jumped up and pawed it, disappointed to find the surface flat. As the board swung and creaked, one of the windows opened and a tousled head poked out.

"Here, you! What are you up to?"

"If this is The Crowned Swan—" Lionel began.

The boy turned a round face to Lionel, blinked several times, and finally replied:

"Seeing as how there's a swan on that signboard; and that swan has a crown on its head, would you say it was The Pig and Whistle?"

"And you're Mistress Gillian?"

The boy blew out his cheeks, rolled up his eyes, and gave a sharp whistle:

"Sure I am. And you're my old granny. I'm Owlbert. And if you can't tell me from Gillian, I'm sorry for you."

Lionel stepped through the door. The large room held only empty tables and benches. No fire burned in the fireplace. As for the finest food in Brightford, he neither saw nor smelled it. Owlbert, a long apron tied around his waist, eyed the puzzled Lionel.

"If you're not Mistress Gillian," said Lionel, "where might I find her? Oh—before I forget, can you tell me: What's a kiss?"

"A kiss?" cried Owlbert. "Now I'm sure you don't have all your wits! What a question!"

"You don't know, either?" Lionel replied.

"Be sure I do!" said Owlbert. At this, he pursed his lips tightly and made loud smacking and chirping noises.

"And that," said Lionel, more perplexed than ever, "that's a kiss?"

"Half of one, you ninny!" retorted Owlbert. "You've got to have someone else for the other half. You don't go kissing alone. You give your part of it— Oh, you're too much for me, I can't make you out. Gillian will have to deal with you herself." He gestured toward the back of the inn. "There you'll see her. And she'll be glad to see you. Oh, just delighted. Tickled pink, you might even say."

Lionel went where the boy pointed. In a room lined with empty shelves, Mistress Gillian sat on a stool behind a trestle table. In front of her lay a sheaf of papers, covered with numbers, which she was studying closely. Lionel remembered Magister Stephanus claiming that humans looked all alike. Stephanus, Lionel decided, was wrong. To begin with, Mistress Gillian had no beard, not even the bluish stubble that covered Swaggart's chin; her face, instead, was smooth. Her dark hair, altogether different from Owlbert's tousled mop, was caught up in the back with a bit of red ribbon. Her sleeves were rolled up to show a pleasantly rounded pair of arms; indeed, all of her seemed agreeably curved and rounded; of the folk he had seen in Brightford, Lionel was sure there was no one else like her.

He had padded up so quietly that Mistress Gillian had not heard him approach. At last, she raised her head. Without seeming too startled at Lionel standing in front of her, she looked squarely at him and demanded:

"Well, who are you? What's your business?"

No judge of a human's years, Lionel guessed that Mistress Gillian, had she been a cat, would have been his own age. Unwrinkled, her forehead and high-arched cheeks were freckled gold and russet. Her hands looked strong and able. "My master calls me Lionel. I don't have any business, but I do have something to give you."

He hesitated. Having neglected to ask Owlbert, he had no idea in the world where to give Mistress Gillian her kiss. Her brow, her cheeks, the end of her nose, the tip of her chin were all within reach and all attractive. Puckering his mouth as Owlbert had shown him, he threw his arms around Gillian's waist and pressed his kiss firmly and loudly on her lips. Delighted at his choice, which seemed the best place of all, Lionel stepped back.

"There," he said. "Now, I'd like some dinner."

Gillian had indeed turned pink, as Owlbert had said she would. She jumped off the stool; but instead of fetching him food, the girl fetched him a stinging box on the ear; then she seized a broom from the corner. Without lingering to learn what had gone amiss, Lionel darted out of the room with Gillian at his heels. He bounded to the shelf above the fireplace, sending cups and tankards flying.

Below, Gillian shook the broom at him and cried:

"I'll dinner you! Oh, I'll roast you one you won't forget!"

"That's what I was hoping," said Lionel.

"Down!" Gillian ordered. "I've not seen you before, but you village gallants are all the same. Strut into Brightford on market day, ogling the girls! You're bold, so long as you're away from home. I've enough on my mind without that. You'll eat a thick slice of humble pie!"

"Pie?" Lionel answered, licking his lips but reluctant to leave his perch. "Yes, if you please. Don't be angry. That's the first I've kissed anyone. If I didn't do it well enough, I'll gladly try again. But everything else is in order. My passport, my license not to keep a dog—"

"The Knave of Clubs?" cried Gillian, as Lionel held out the pieces of pasteboard. "The King of Diamonds? Oh, I'll deal you a different hand!"

"Is there something wrong with these?" Lionel asked. "When Master Swaggart sold them to me—"

"Swaggart? Sold? What are you talking about?"

"He kindly let me buy them," Lionel said, explaining how matters had turned out so well for him. "I'm much obliged to him. I don't want to break any of your laws. It took all my money, but I was lucky to have enough."

"Are you really such a fool?" Gillian asked. "If Swaggart sold you these, he plucked you like a pigeon!"

"He couldn't," said Lionel. "I'm a cat."

"Don't sauce me!" cried Gillian, shaking the broom. "I'm in no mood for nonsense."

"It's true," Lionel insisted. "I was my master's cat. He changed me into a human."

"I had an uncle who thought he was a horse," put in Owlbert, who had been listening to this exchange. "Ate and slept standing up, he did. And always asking to be hitched to a wagon."

"Cat, are you?" Gillian burst out. "Then, scat!"

"You'd better run home," agreed Owlbert. "Ask your master to put down a saucer of milk. Don't wander around Brightford telling folk you're a cat. There's only two things can happen. Either they believe you or they don't. Them as don't believe you, they'll want to lock you away. Them as do believe you, they might try drowning you in a bucket of water."

At a loss, Lionel was about to jump down; but he crouched warily as the inn door opened with a clatter and he glimpsed a short, round-bellied man, bald except for a few strings of gray hair. His dark robe was stained and wrinkled, shiny with wear. From his back, the newcomer unstrapped a large chest of polished wood fitted with dozens of drawers and cubbyholes; then he mopped his brow and ruddy cheeks with a grimy square of linen.

"*Bona fides,*" he declared briskly. "That is, as we say in the *lingua medica,* good day to one and all—and what's that one doing on the mantelpiece?"

"He's a cat," replied Owlbert. "So he says; and he should know."

"*Cattus domesticus?*" asked the newcomer. "He's an odd-looking breed, then. I'd certainly have taken him for a young man."

"He is," Gillian said, "and I've neither time nor mind for his foolishness. And no patience with peddlers, either."

"Peddler? Indeed not!" the stranger answered. "*Medicus illustrius! Ne plus ultra!* You may address me simply as: Dr. Tudbelly."

CHAPTER VII

The Illustrious Dr. Tudbelly and His Armamentarium

❧ "*O tempora, O mores,*" Dr. Tudbelly went on. "I've come in the nick of time. Clearly, this poor fellow suffers from an attack of *delusionis cattibus*. A common malady. I see it frequently in my travels."

Deftly, he undid a number of brass hooks at the bottom of the wooden chest; four legs dropped down to form a table. He attached another section, making a narrow counter on which he set a pestle and mortar and a number of bottles and beakers from one of the compartments.

"My Armamentarium," Dr. Tudbelly proudly declared. "Thanks to its unique resources, I am able to make available a complete selection of elixirs, tinctures, and unguents for man or beast. First, however, if I might find the innkeeper and pay my respects to him—"

"To her, you mean," said Owlbert. "There Gillian stands in front of you."

"Mistress innkeeper," Dr. Tudbelly said, bowing grandly, "you are a fortunate young woman; especially if you happen to be suffering from hives, warts, indigestion, falling hair, tremulous dropsy—"

"I suffer from fools and rogues," Gillian replied. "They make my head ache. As it aches right now."

"*Dolus cranius?* Excellent!" Dr. Tudbelly beamed in satisfaction. "*Fiat lux*—you're in luck. Allow me to offer you an infusion of *Panacea Tudbellia*. In layman's terms: Tudbelly's Universal Cure-All. A priceless medicament. You, however, shall have it absolutely free of charge— ah, that is, in exchange for a night's lodging and a modest repast in your *refectorium*."

"First a joker, now a charlatan!" Gillian threw up her hands. "Out! Out! There's nothing here for you, not even if you had money to pay for it."

"That's right," Owlbert put in glumly. "We're on short rations ourselves. And that pinches. Especially me, as I'm like to grow up all stunted without my proper victuals."

"What's this?" Dr. Tudbelly asked. "An inn where the innkeeper and potboy go hungry?"

Lionel, meantime, had cautiously jumped down from the shelf. "Master Swaggart told me you served the best food in Brightford."

"So I do," Gillian returned. "Or, so I did. My inn's shut down. There's hardly a crust in my cupboard, thanks to Mayor Pursewig."

"When I was a kitten," said Lionel, "Magister Stephanus used to complain I'd eat him out of house and home. This fellow Earwig—or Pursemouth, whatever you called him—did he do that to you? He must have an appetite!"

"For gold, yes!" retorted Gillian. "The greedy money-grubber! He owns the bridge, the toll gate, and mortgages on half the houses in town. Now he wants to gobble up The Crowned Swan. Since my father died, Pursewig's done everything to ruin my trade and drive me out of business. He'd have me quit and give up the inn to him. I've fought him all I can," she went on bitterly, "but the way things have gone, sooner or later he'll get what he wants."

"He's had Swaggart and his crew break our windows," added Owlbert. "They've smashed our crockery, stuffed rags down the chimney—"

"Yes, and with what it cost to mend the damage," said Gillian, "I haven't a penny left to buy meat or drink. I can't borrow anywhere. The only moneylender is Pursewig! The tradesmen don't dare give me credit; they're all in debt to Pursewig. So, my inn's closed; and no way to open it again. What good's an eating house with nothing to eat in it?"

"What it comes down to," said Owlbert, "is if you want food, you'll have to go and scratch for it."

"Scratch?" said Lionel. "Gladly!"

"Do it, then!" Gillian challenged. "I'll strike you two a bargain. Bring me something to cook, and I'll cook it for you. Whatever it is, you have my word: I'll make it the tastiest dish you'll find in Brightford or anywhere else."

"I'll help you eat it, too," said Owlbert. "You have my word on that."

Dr. Tudbelly rubbed his paunch. *"Carpe diem*—I haven't even had a morsel of fish today. Well, young man, it would seem that you and I are in the same predicament. Come along, then, if you want to fill your stomach. I shall entrust my Armamentarium to the excellent care of Mistress Gillian until we return; which, I assure you, will be *postum hastum*. I advise this alert, intelligent young gentleman to light a good fire meanwhile; and make sure the pots and pans are ready."

With that, Dr. Tudbelly bowed once more and stepped briskly from the inn, Lionel following him. Outside, the illustrious doctor glanced up and down the street.

"Now, my boy, our first task is to find the local purveyor of meat."

"That's easy," answered Lionel, raising his head and sniffing. He beckoned to Dr. Tudbelly. "It's this way."

"Nosce tempus—that's quite a nose you have," Dr. Tudbelly said in admiration as Lionel unhesitatingly led him around one corner, then another, to an open-fronted stall where a man in a white apron was busily carving a side of beef. "Now, leave the rest to me."

"I don't think he'll give you any meat unless you give him money," Lionel warned. "That seems to be the way of things in Brightford."

"There's more than one way to skin a cat," said Dr. Tudbelly, immediately adding, "An unfortunate phrase. Forgive me."

Smiling confidently, Dr. Tudbelly strode to the butcher. "Good day, sir. On behalf of Mistress Gillian, I have the pleasure to request your company as an honored guest for dinner."

"What, is The Crowned Swan open again?" replied the butcher.

"It will be," Dr. Tudbelly assured him, "this very day. And you, I trust, will be on hand to join the festivities. Mistress Gillian is going to cook a delicious *Pro Bono Publico*. And you, sir, of course you know how splendidly she prepares that. My mouth already waters!"

"So does mine!" cried the butcher. "Oh, I'll be there! Count on it! I can't wait to taste that *Pro Bono*—ah, whatever you said."

"Since you bring up the subject of bones," Dr. Tudbelly replied, "there's one thing needed to make the dish absolutely perfect. Some good, rich marrow bones. Alas, Mistress Gillian has none in her kitchen. But no matter, she'll manage without them."

"And spoil the dish for lack of a bone?" returned the butcher. "Indeed not! I'll bring her a whole basketful."

"Excellent! And some chickens, too, if you happen to think of it—to flavor the sauce," said Dr. Tudbelly, leaving the delighted butcher already starting to fill a hamper.

With Lionel beside him, Dr. Tudbelly hustled down the street. "Now, my boy, see if you can find a vegetable stand for us."

"This way," said Lionel, guiding the illustrious doctor. "I can smell carrots and cabbages—and onions, too."

"*Nostrilus miraculus!* What a marvelous sniffer!" Dr. Tudbelly exclaimed. "How did you learn that trick?"

"It's easy," answered Lionel. "Any cat can do it."

"Oh—ah, yes; to be sure, to be sure," Dr. Tudbelly agreed, approaching the vegetable stand Lionel had found with no difficulty.

Here, the illustrious doctor gave the vegetable seller the same invitation as the butcher, and received the same eager acceptance. This time, however, Dr. Tudbelly added:

"I'm afraid, though, Mistress Gillian's run short of parsley. And that's the secret of the whole recipe. Oh, the dish will be tasty enough without it. Not quite so good, of course. But it will do."

"If that's all she needs," answered the vegetable seller, "I'll give her parsley by the armload!"

"Or was it onions?" Dr. Tudbelly frowned and scratched his chin. "No, I'm sure it was—turnips. Though it might have been carrots. Or green beans?"

"If you can't remember which," replied the vegetable seller, "then I'd better bring some of each."

"Splendid thought!" Dr. Tudbelly cried. "By all means! While you're at it, you might as well fill a couple of sacks, just to make sure there's enough."

Lionel's nose led him next to the bakery. There, the baker was delighted at the invitation to Gillian's feast. However, Dr. Tudbelly raised a cautioning finger:

"Don't be disappointed. I must, in all frankness, tell you I don't think Mistress Gillian has enough bread. You won't be able to sop up the gravy. Alas, that's the best part of her *Pro Bono Publico*."

"Oh, I wouldn't want to miss that gravy," said the baker, licking his lips and rubbing his flour-daubed hands. "Bread? I'll bring enough to sop up a whole sea of gravy!"

"A few cakes and pies might come in handy, too," Dr. Tudbelly remarked. "A dozen or so should be enough."

From the bake shop, Lionel led Dr. Tudbelly to the brewery, where the illustrious doctor tendered the same invitation, adding:

"Mistress Gillian's *Pro Bono Publico* will be delicious, naturally. Though perhaps a little weak, without a drop of ale to give it zest."

"A drop of ale for seasoning?" exclaimed the burly brewer. "Once it's tapped, I might as well bring along the whole barrel!"

The fishwife, the dairymaid, and the wine merchant were all as quick and eager to accept the invitation as the other tradesmen; and, like the others, gladly offered to bring all that Dr. Tudbelly suggested and more. At last, the illustrious doctor and Lionel hurried back to The Crowned Swan.

There, Owlbert greeted them with arms outstretched. "Here, let me help you with all the good things you're bringing. Where are you hiding them? In your pockets? Too much for you to carry? I guess we can expect every tradesman in town to come delivering food."

"We've invited them all, and they'll be here any moment," Lionel assured Owlbert. He went quickly to Gillian. "Dr. Tudbelly promised you'd cook a *Pro Bono Publico* for them."

"A what?" cried Gillian. "What have you pair of rascals been up to? I told you there's not enough in my larder to cook anything, let alone a—a whatever-it-is!"

"In layman's terms, a stew," replied Dr. Tudbelly. "Believe me, you'll have all you need."

CHAPTER VIII

The Company at The Crowned Swan

◦ "But we forgot something," said Lionel in sudden dismay. "Mayor Pursewig! We should invite him. If he's as greedy as you say, he'll surely want to come."

"Yes, to spoil whatever he can," Gillian answered. "He's the biggest rogue in Brightford. Let him set foot here! I'll pepper him!"

Before Gillian could say more, Owlbert pointed excitedly into the street. Hurrying toward the inn came the butcher, the vegetable seller, the baker, and all the rest, carrying hampers and sacks, or trundling barrows overflowing with provisions.

Gillian ran to welcome these unexpected arrivals, urging them to be patient while she prepared their feast. Owlbert hastily filled tankards; Lionel and Dr. Tudbelly, forgetting their own dinners, set to work at top speed, peeling potatoes, chopping cabbages, and slicing carrots. Gillian stirred half a dozen pots, tasted their contents, added seasoning, and somehow managed to be everywhere at once. By the time her stew had simmered to perfection, the eating room was packed with townspeople; not only the invited tradesmen, but paying guests as well, for word had spread that The Crowned Swan was open again. Even the town musicians came; and, hearing the lively tunes, partners jumped up from the tables, flung their arms around each other, and began whirling as fast as they could go.

"Stop them!" cried Lionel. "They'll hurt themselves!"

"Not likely!" Gillian laughed good-naturedly at Lionel's alarm. "Have you never danced? Come on, then, I'll show you how."

Leaving her stew pots and taking hold of the astonished Lionel, Gillian led him skipping and spinning around the room. Lionel quickly learned to match his steps to the music; and in no time he and Gillian were dancing more lightly and gracefully than any couple in the room.

Suddenly the music stopped. The door had burst open. The merrymakers fell silent. Drawing away from Lionel, Gillian put her hands on her hips and, looking squarely at the new arrival, declared:

"What, His Honor Mayor Pursewig? Come to savor the feast?"

Lionel, to his surprise, saw a spindle-shanked, narrow-shouldered little man with a sallow face, a sharp nose, and a mouth puckered like a prune. He wore a red robe trimmed all around with fur, and from his shriveled neck hung a heavy chain of gleaming yellow metal.

"You? Mayor Pursewig?" said Lionel, stepping closer and examining this personage with great curiosity. "The biggest rogue in Brightford? You look the smallest!"

Pursewig's jaw dropped. His nose twitched, his cheeks grew mottled, and he could squeeze out no answer beyond a stifled clucking and gasping.

"There's not much meat on you, either," Lionel went on. "Shouldn't you be fatter, if you're so greedy? And that chain—it must be very heavy around your neck. Is it gold? Do you really have an appetite for it? You should try Mistress Gillian's *Pro Bono Publico*. It's tastier."

The townsfolk burst into laughter. Pursewig at last found voice enough to sputter:

"Insolent whelp! Impertinent puppy!"

"Puppy?" Lionel protested. "Anything but!"

"Out of my way!" commanded Pursewig, stepping into the eating room, where he stood glaring at Mistress Gillian and the company. "Just as I suspected. I knew what I'd find here. A meeting place for every idle tongue in Brightford!"

"Indeed?" retorted Gillian. "Yours is the only idle tongue here."

"Impudent girl!" cried Pursewig. "Your inn's a nest of troublemakers and malcontents!" He stretched his neck as far as it would go above his fur-trimmed collar and peered into the crowd. "You there! Oh, I see you, Master Tolliver!"

Pursewig looked as if he might choke on his own

words, and his face went livid as he pointed at still another guest, a gray-haired man in a dark jacket and well-tailored cloak. "And you, Master Fuller! A Town Councilman! For shame, consorting with these ne'er-do-wells!"

"Shame?" replied Master Fuller in a calm voice, looking Pursewig straight in the eye. "See to your own behavior, sir, before you speak of shame to others."

"Be silent!" Pursewig snapped. "I'll deal with you in Council Meeting. And you, mistress, your score will be settled, as well." He turned and called, "Swaggart! Clear the inn!"

"This is atrocious," Master Fuller declared, rising to his feet as Swaggart and a company of Watchmen armed with crossbows shouldered their way into the room. "You have no right—"

"I have every right," Pursewig retorted, "and every duty to disperse these ruffians and rascals!"

Pursewig turned on his heel and stamped from the room. Protesting angrily, the guests could do no more than obey the Watchmen, who prodded them out of The Crowned Swan.

"And what have we here?" called Swaggart, catching sight of Lionel. "Master Puss again? Run home or you'll get your tail stepped on."

"Mistress Gillian says you plucked me like a pigeon," Lionel replied. "I think that means you took away my money. If you please, I'd like it back. I don't have any use for it, but Gillian might find something to do with it."

42

"For a village idiot, you're a brazen one," Swaggart returned. "Your money back? Here, I'll give you something better!"

At that, Swaggart aimed a blow at Lionel's head. Quick though Swaggart was, Lionel's sharp eyes had already caught what his opponent intended and he stepped easily away. Enraged at this agility, crimson-faced, Swaggart made to throw himself bodily upon Lionel, who vaulted over a table and landed lightly on his feet. Swaggart went pitching head over heels.

"*Magna cum laude!*" called Dr. Tudbelly, seeing Lionel more than able to defend himself. "Well done, my boy!"

Swaggart sat up, rubbing his neck and glaring at Lionel. He climbed to one knee and his hand darted to his sash. In one motion, he snatched out a short-bladed knife and threw it straight at Lionel's throat.

Again, Lionel dodged. The blade missed its mark, but grazed the side of his head, and he stumbled backwards, crying out as much in shock as pain. Swaggart scrambled to regain the weapon, shoving aside Dr. Tudbelly, who had come to Lionel's aid.

However, before Swaggart seized his blade, Gillian seized her broom; she belabored him as if he had been her own floor in need of a sweeping. Bawling, clutching his head, Swaggart dashed out the door with Gillian behind him, launching a last drubbing to send him faster on his way.

Lionel, meantime, had clambered to his feet. He stared

at the knife. "A thing like that can be dangerous. Swaggart should have been more careful."

"If he'd been more careful," remarked Owlbert, crawling from under one of the tables, where he had been observing the dispute, "he'd have stuck you right in the windpipe."

"Why—why, that would have killed me!" Lionel exclaimed.

"It wouldn't lead to a ripe old age," said Owlbert. "What did you think he was trying to do?"

Lionel's jaw dropped in horror. "Do the folk of Brightford kill their own kind? That's worse than Stephanus told me! These creatures are monsters!"

"Alas, very commonplace," Dr. Tudbelly said. "If you're surprised at people trying to do away with each other, I think you must be a cat! Or else that cut on your head is deeper than it looks. Here, my boy, drink this," he added, handing Lionel a glass of amber liquid from the Armamentarium. "It will set you on your feet again."

No sooner did he swallow it than Lionel's legs buckled and he tumbled to the floor. Gillian flung away the broom and knelt at his side.

"Idiot!" she cried to the illustrious doctor. "What have you done to him?"

"Ah—well, it would seem," replied Dr. Tudbelly, puzzled at the effect of his own potion, "*Tonicus Tubellius*—some small error in the recipe. It's turned out to be soothing syrup. But never fear. *Sic transit gloria mundi*. A transient illness; he'll be fine tomorrow."

For all his efforts, Lionel could not regain his feet. Gillian lifted his head to her lap and gently stroked his brow. Forgetting his discomfort, Lionel smiled happily.

"He's choking!" Gillian cried in alarm.

"I'm purring," murmured Lionel.

"Enough!" Gillian burst out. "Next thing, you'll have me believing you really are a cat! And I, like a great fool, sit here petting you! Owlbert! Dr. Tudbelly! Get him to bed before he takes the notion of prowling the rooftops!"

Lionel had shut his eyes, quite content for Gillian to stroke his head. He opened them again to find himself tucked under a goose-feather quilt in a small bedchamber. He started up, and put his hands to his throbbing temples. Through the window, he glimpsed the first streaks of dawn.

"Magister Stephanus! He'll be furious with me!"

He climbed out of bed and fumbled at the leather pouch around his neck. He stopped at the sound of footfalls in the yard below. Head still spinning from Dr. Tudbelly's potion, Lionel stumbled to the window. He leaned out in time to catch sight of shadowy figures, a dozen or more, each carrying what appeared to be empty sacks. He rubbed his eyes. The figures, he now recognized, were Town Watchmen. In another moment, they vanished.

Wondering whether the illustrious doctor's medication had made his eyes play tricks on him, Lionel closed up the leather pouch. Curiosity aroused, he first decided to climb through the window and jump down into the inn yard. Instead, fuddled by the potion, he had strength only to stagger back to the bed.

It was full daylight when he woke again. He yawned, stretched his arms and legs, snuffled comfortably, and licked his lips at the prospect of the bowl of warm milk Stephanus always put out for him. Then he sat upright, remembering who and where he was.

He jumped to his feet, hurried out of the chamber and down a flight of steps. He found Gillian in the kitchen, her hair disheveled, her cheeks smudged.

"Well, you look in better state than you were," Gillian said to him. "If only I could say as much for The Crowned Swan. We have some new guests."

"The Town Watchmen?" Lionel asked. "The ones I saw in the yard this morning? They were carrying bags, but they didn't stay long."

"So that's it!" Gillian burst out. "I knew Pursewig had a hand in it. And Swaggart, too. Those villains must have worked half the night! I wish you were a cat! They've filled my cellar with rats!"

CHAPTER IX

The Battle in the Cellar

ぐ "Rats?" Lionel pricked up his ears and his eyes brightened.

"By the score! By the hundreds!" Gillian cried angrily. "More than I can ever deal with! They're in the cellar now; next, they'll be in the larder, the pantry, the kitchen, and every room in the house."

"Not at all, my dear young woman," put in Dr. Tudbelly, who had awakened and come down the stairs in time to hear Gillian's outburst. "My Armamentarium will provide the means of ridding your hostelry of this undesirable infestation without another moment's delay. After which, if you were to insist, I should be glad to accept something *sub specie breakfastus*."

"Don't trouble yourself," said Lionel. "I may not know about kissing, but I do know about rats."

"No trouble whatever," Dr. Tudbelly replied, pouring the contents of several drawers into a mixing bowl and stirring briskly. "A simple preparation of *Rattus Extermi-*

natus Tudbellius, known far and wide as Tudbelly's Rat Bane."

From a pigeonhole in the Armamentarium, the learned doctor produced a vial of green liquid, unstoppered it, and poured a quantity into the bowl. Immediately, the mixture began hissing and steaming, bubbling, boiling, and spouting like a volcano. It overflowed the container, drenching the illustrious Tudbelly from head to foot before he could throw the concoction to the floor.

Owlbert shouted in alarm. Lionel and Gillian, fearing Dr. Tudbelly had scalded himself, ran to help. The learned doctor was unharmed; but his robe, which had been stained and wrinkled, was now spotless, without the slightest trace of dirt or grime. The creases were gone; the garment looked as if it never had been worn.

Some of Dr. Tudbelly's mixture had also spattered Lionel's boots. These now gleamed with a lustrous polish; the leather had suddenly grown softer, suppler, and more comfortable than ever.

"That's good, that is," muttered Owlbert. "We'll have the cleanest rats in Brightford."

"Show me the cellar," Lionel urged Gillian, who had turned away in disappointment. "Believe me, I'll have those rats out of there in no time."

"You can't do any worse, that's for sure," Gillian sighed. Taking Lionel by the hand, she led him through the kitchen to a heavy wooden door, which she cautiously opened. She lit a candle, gave it to Lionel, and pointed down a flight of stone steps.

Lionel eagerly made his way into the cellar. But there he halted warily. Perched on casks and barrels, scampering over the bottle racks, in and out of corners, squealing and squeaking, were even more of the beady-eyed creatures than he had expected.

At sight of Lionel, some of the rats stood on their hind legs, raised their snouts, and bared their needle-sharp teeth, daring him to venture closer.

He glared at this horde for a moment. Their stench made his nostrils twitch. His heart began to leap and pound. He drew back his lips and clenched his teeth. From deep in his throat came a low, threatening growl that rose higher and higher. Every muscle taut, he crouched and thrust his head forward. Then he sprang.

Heedless of the snapping jaws, he seized one of the biggest rats, shook it furiously, and sent it flying through the air, then plunged after the others. Forgetting Stephanus had changed him into a man, Lionel spat and hissed in rage. His eyes blazed; his hands seemed to bristle again with claws. Yowling a battle cry, he slashed about him right and left.

The squealing of the rats became shrieks of terror. The creatures dashed for the steps, nipping at each other's tails and paws in a mad scramble to escape this giant cat. They pelted up the stairs, through pantry and kitchen, through the eating room into the street, with Lionel roaring after them.

Seeing this fleeing army streaking over the cobbles, housewives dropped their market baskets and ran screaming, while others stared openmouthed, clutching their skirts and aprons. The tailor gaped from his shop window. The hatter slammed his shutters. The vegetable seller tumbled backwards into his baskets of greens.

Lionel had no thoughts for Gillian, Brightford, Dr. Tudbelly, or even Magister Stephanus as he bounded after the rats. His blood was up, and he wanted nothing more than to sink his teeth into his enemies. Owlbert, who had taken up the pursuit along with him, glanced fearfully at the raging Lionel.

Instead of spreading through the town, the stream of rats held its course. For now all the cats in Brightford had come to join the chase. Black cats, white cats, tabbies, tortoiseshells, ginger-colored, bob-tailed, long-tailed, they raced along on both sides, forcing the rats to keep straight ahead.

At last, Lionel's calm returned. Leaving his helpers to continue the chase, he turned back to The Crowned Swan.

"There!" he triumphantly cried to Gillian. "I told you I'd get rid of those fellows!"

Before the astonished Gillian could reply, Dr. Tudbelly clapped Lionel on the shoulder.

"Magnificent! Why, there was a moment when I really thought you'd grow a tail and whiskers! My boy, you can make a fortune from that skill. I've nothing in my Armamentarium to match it. I'll hire you here and now as a first-class rat catcher."

Owlbert, by this time, had given up the chase and

now came running into The Crowned Swan. "The rats! What they've done—"

"They're not back again?" asked Lionel. "They wouldn't dare!"

"Oh, they're gone, all right," Owlbert replied. "Every last one. Gone, all of them. Into Pursewig's house!"

CHAPTER X

Lionel Says Farewell

⋖⋗ "The best place for them!" cried Lionel, delighted at having done Gillian another good turn.

"He'll think twice before he tries more of his tricks," Gillian said, looking admiringly at Lionel. "Call yourself a cat? I'd say you're a tiger!"

"After exertions like yours," put in Dr. Tudbelly, "there is always the danger of *gastribus flaccibus*—that is to say, pernicious hunger. Left untreated, it leads to a severe case of *corpus delictus*. In fact, I fear I may be suffering from it myself."

"Come on, then," said Gillian. "I'll feed you. We all need breakfast after a morning like this."

From the feast of the night before, there were only leftovers: the remains of a chicken, some bread and cheese. Dr. Tudbelly, eager to avoid the dangers he had warned against, gave all his attention to emptying his plate and filling his paunch. Lionel, to his surprise, had no appetite.

"Magister Stephanus must wonder what's become of me," he said. "I gave my word I'd come home without delay. Now, I suppose I'll have to be on my way."

"If that's what you must do," Gillian said regretfully, "I won't ask you to stay, much as I'd like to. Besides, Pursewig and Swaggart have scores to settle with you. The sooner you leave Brightford, the safer you'll be."

"Those two scoundrels can't be too fond of me, either," said Dr. Tudbelly. "We both had better depart *quickissimus*. If Swaggart sets the Town Watch after us, though, it won't be easy."

"For me, it would be," said Lionel. "Magister Stephanus is a wizard. Before I left, he gave me a wishbone."

"That was generous of him, wasn't it?" put in Owlbert.

"He told me if I was ever in trouble to break it and wish myself home again," Lionel went on, "and I'd be there in that same instant."

"No offense intended," Dr. Tudbelly said, "but I might question where your master served his apprenticeship. No doubt with some provincial alchemist or country sorcerer. Any qualified thaumaturge knows that such a thing is impossible. A wishbone? To transport—ah, no, my boy, that's ridiculous! What you must really have is a *patella funicularis*—the kneecap of a phoenix."

"I'm sure you know about such things," Lionel answered respectfully, "but I can't believe my master would give me a wishbone that didn't work."

"To send you flying through the air?" Gillian frowned. "That's a new fancy you've got into your head. Perhaps, after all, you'd better stay here and rest a little longer. I don't think you're well enough to travel anywhere."

"The matter is easily settled," Dr. Tudbelly said. "Let me scrutinize the item in question. I can tell at a glance if it's genuine."

Lionel undid his collar and reached into the leather pouch. Then he gasped. It was empty.

"The wishbone's gone!" he cried, jumping to his feet. Desperately he searched his pockets, the folds of his clothing, even his boot tops. Dropping to hands and knees, he began picking his way across the floor, sniffing and peering into every cranny.

"We'd better humor him," Dr. Tudbelly whispered to Gillian, and gestured for Owlbert to make a show of helping the search. "In my opinion, he's suffering from *illusionis wishbonis.* I shall compound an antidotal electuary."

However, the illustrious doctor had scarcely time to open a drawer of the Armamentarium when Owlbert called out:

"Here it is!"

Lionel gratefully took the wishbone from Owlbert's hand and was about to pass the talisman to Dr. Tudbelly. But the illustrious doctor and Gillian were staring at the open doorway and the furious figure of Mayor Pursewig.

The spindle-shanked Mayor still wore his nightcap; he had thrown his robes of office over a nightshirt that dragged at his heels; his gold chain hung askew; and his fur-trimmed slippers nearly flew off his feet as he made straight for Lionel.

"You!" shrilled Pursewig, hopping with rage. "You put rats in my house! To chew up everything in sight! The food in my larder! Sacks of malt! Sides of bacon! All! All! But I'll have it out of you. Every penny! I'll have a judgment against you. Damages! Fines! Penalties!"

"Wretched little man," exclaimed Gillian, "get out of my inn! Damages? Judgments? Take the rats to court!"

"Gently, sir, gently," put in Dr. Tudbelly, as Pursewig's nose trembled and his cheeks flapped in and out like a broken bellows. "You'll bring an *apoplexia* on yourself. *Dies irae*—don't lose your temper so early in the day. Now, sir, allow me to count your *pulsus*."

So saying, the illustrious Tudbelly took Pursewig's wrist with one hand and with the other tried to pry open the Mayor's mouth. "Your tongue, sir. Oblige me by protruding it. Ah, just as I suspected: a fulminating biliosity. But never fear! I have the remedy."

Pursewig tore his wrist away from Dr. Tudbelly, thrust the learned doctor aside, and shook a fist at Lionel. "I'll have you in a cell! For years!"

"I'm sorry," Lionel replied, "I couldn't let you do that. My master would really lose patience with me."

Raging at this apparent impudence, Pursewig flung himself on Lionel, who quickly put out a hand to ward off the attack, seizing the first thing he could grasp: the Mayor's nose. And thus he held his kicking, struggling assailant at arm's length.

"Assault! Battery! Grievous bodily harm!" shrieked Pursewig. "Help! Swaggart! Swaggart!"

Dr. Tudbelly, opening a drawer of the Armamentarium, removed several tubes, fitted them together, inserted a plunger at one end and a sharp-pointed cap at the other.

Mayor Pursewig, glimpsing Dr. Tudbelly approaching armed with such a device, gave a final burst of strength, broke free of Lionel's grip, stumbled through the door and into the street, bawling for Swaggart, the Town Watch, the Town Council, and the Brightford Fire Guards.

"Lionel, he meant what he said!" cried Gillian. "He'll have you in prison—or worse. Don't wait another instant. Go! Now!"

Dr. Tudbelly and Owlbert urged the same. Lionel nodded reluctantly:

"If all of you think it's best—" He turned to Gillian. "Before I go, if you don't mind I'd like to try that kiss again."

Without waiting for the girl's answer, Lionel suited his action to his words. Gillian turned as pink as she had done before. Lionel braced himself for the expected box on the ear. This time there was none.

"Farewell, friends," Lionel said. "I'll be glad to see the last of Brightford. But I'm sorry to leave you, just when I'm getting the knack of this matter of kissing—"

"Dr. Tudbelly, go with him and don't let him out of your sight until he's safe wherever he belongs," Gillian said. "Alone, he'll get himself into some new pickle."

"No need," said Lionel, holding up the wishbone. "I have this. I'll be home in an instant."

He stepped back, shut his eyes tightly, wished himself once more with Magister Stephanus, and snapped the bone in two.

Next moment, he opened his eyes to blink, dumbfounded. He had not budged an inch from where he stood.

Dr. Tudbelly Finishes Breakfast

ૐ✎ Dazed, Lionel stared at the fragments in his hand. Gillian shook him by the shoulders:

"Now will you listen to me?" She turned to Dr. Tudbelly. "Get him out of Brightford. Anywhere. Hurry!"

"Here's Swaggart," warned Owlbert, who had been leaning out a window of the eating room. "Pursewig's with him, and half the Town Watch, besides."

Dr. Tudbelly hastily gathered up the leftovers from the table, stuffed them into the Armamentarium, and hoisted the cabinet onto his back. Gillian seized the baffled Lionel, spun him around, and pushed him through the kitchen, where she hustled him out a back doorway into a narrow alley.

"What went wrong?" stammered Lionel. "Magister Stephanus told me—"

"*Vita brevis!*" Dr. Tudbelly exclaimed. "Run for your life!"

With a last backward glance at Gillian, Lionel let the illustrious doctor pull him along. The two clattered through the alley: Lionel despairing over the useless wishbone, Dr. Tudbelly puffing under the weight of his Armamentarium. Though faster on his feet than Lionel would have supposed, Dr. Tudbelly soon began to falter; his pudgy cheeks flushed, and he gasped painfully for breath. Seeing his companion's difficulty, Lionel halted, lifted the Armamentarium from the shoulders of the learned doctor, and strapped it onto his own back. They set off again with Dr. Tudbelly, greatly relieved, pumping his short legs to keep pace with Lionel's loping strides.

Without troubling to think where he was heading, Lionel let his sense of direction guide him. Though he knew little about Brightford, he raced along, somehow sure of his bearings and where he meant to go. After a short while, he saw the market place ahead, and Brightford Bridge at the far side of it.

"We'll cross," he cried to Dr. Tudbelly. "It's the quickest way out of Brightford."

Then his hackles rose and his eyes widened. While Swaggart had led one company of Watchmen to the inn, he had left another to patrol the square. Dragging Dr. Tudbelly after him, summoning all his strength for a burst of speed, Lionel dashed to the bridge. The Watchmen, shouting for the fugitives to halt, ran toward them.

"The toll gate!" Dr. Tudbelly groaned at the sight of the barrier and its sharp spikes. "We're caught!"

"Jump it!" returned Lionel. "Over and away!"

"You're the cat, not I!" Dr. Tudbelly protested. "Go on, my boy. Do it if you can."

Realizing it was hopeless to expect the portly doctor to leap the barrier or even climb over it, Lionel fell back in dismay. The guards at the bridge raised their crossbows. Behind the fugitives, the Watchmen were scrambling across the market place and would be upon them in another moment.

Lionel cringed as he glanced at the river. Then, clenching his teeth, he hoisted Dr. Tudbelly to the wall of the bridge, clambered up beside him, and sent him tumbling into the water below. Shutting his eyes, hunching his shoulders, Lionel followed the plummeting doctor and pitched headlong into the river.

Choking, terrified that his lungs would burst, Lionel paddled with his hands and kicked back and forth trying to untangle himself from the Armamentarium. At last free of the harness, he glimpsed Dr. Tudbelly's glistening pate bobbing beside him. The Armamentarium had floated to the surface, and the two hapless swimmers clung to it.

Bolts from the crossbows whistled past Lionel's ears. However, before the Watchmen could reload, the swift current had borne the Armamentarium downstream, well out of range. Dr. Tudbelly, puffing and wheezing, flung an arm over the wooden cabinet and with the other tried to paddle landward.

"*Terra firma!*" sputtered the illustrious doctor. "Pull for shore!"

Lionel obeyed, thrashing and scooping at the water. But the Armamentarium sped along, and it was all the two unwilling sailors could do to keep their handholds.

Past a bend in the river, the water turned shallow. Lionel's toes scraped bottom, and at last he and Dr. Tudbelly were able to guide the cabinet to the riverbank and haul it ashore. There, Dr. Tudbelly hurriedly and anxiously examined the drawers and compartments. Satisfied that his precious Armamentarium had stayed watertight and none the worse for serving as a raft, Dr. Tudbelly collapsed flat on his back.

"*Aqua vitae!*" he cried, blowing out his breath. "The river saved our lives!"

Shuddering as much with distaste as with chill, Lionel shook himself from head to foot, then crouched on the pebbles, dabbed away the water from his face, and rubbed at his water-filled ears.

"I've never been so wet in all my life," he moaned. "I've never gone swimming before, either; and I don't mean to do it again."

"Be thankful you don't have to," replied Dr. Tudbelly. "We're safely out of Brightford. Find your way to Dunstan Forest, and your troubles are over."

"Yes—I suppose they are," Lionel answered with some hesitation. "But what about Gillian's?"

"She's a girl of spirit," Dr. Tudbelly assured him. "She'll manage, one way or another."

"I hope so," answered Lionel. "But somehow—I wish I hadn't left her. And yet, I promised Magister Stephanus I'd come home directly. I'm sure he never thought I'd be gone so long. I don't know what to do. It all feels mixed up in my head—"

"Merely a normal state of affairs," Dr. Tudbelly replied, getting to his stocky legs. "Everything is more confusing on an empty stomach. *Natura abhoret vacuo.* I dislike having my breakfast interrupted. It produces palpitations of the jejunum."

Opening a compartment of the Armamentarium, Dr. Tudbelly took out the leftovers he had salvaged from the inn: the remains of chicken and some bread crusts.

"Here," he said cheerfully, offering half to Lionel. "You'd better have something. You look a little green around the gills."

"Gills?" cried Lionel, clapping his hands to his neck. "Am I turning into a fish?"

"Only a manner of speaking," Dr. Tudbelly said. "Eat, my boy. It's the best way to ward off splenetic chilblains."

Lionel shook his head. "I'm not hungry."

"A bad sign," said Dr. Tudbelly. "But I have just the thing for you in the Armamentarium. I'll attend to it in a moment."

With that, Dr. Tudbelly attacked his portion of chicken so hastily that he began to choke. He rolled his eyes and pointed desperately at his throat.

Lionel hurried to oblige the strangling Tudbelly by pounding him on the back. In another moment, after a racking cough, the offending morsel shot from the doctor's gullet and fell to the pebbles.

It was a wishbone.

CHAPTER XII

Lionel Finds His Wishbone and Loses His Way

❊✍ "Ah, what a relief! Thank you, my boy. There's a lesson: *Festina lente*—never bolt your food." Having caught his breath and wiped the tears from his eyes, Dr. Tudbelly turned to his meal again.

Lionel, seeing what the illustrious doctor had nearly swallowed, snatched up the wishbone:

"This is the one! The one Stephanus gave me—it must be!"

"I should hardly think so," answered Dr. Tudbelly, between mouthfuls. "Mistress Gillian's chicken is delicious, I admit, but not one to have enchanted bones, gizzards, or whatever."

Lionel turned the wishbone back and forth in his fingers. "It must have fallen out while I was running through the kitchen after the rats, and got mixed in the rest of the food. Here, see how dry it is, and so carefully polished."

Dr. Tudbelly studied Lionel's find and, after some

long moments, nodded his head. "Yes, a fresh fowl would hardly come equipped with an old bone. Well, there you have it. But if indeed it has the transportational properties you claim, there's only one way to prove it. Break the thing and see what happens. Wish yourself home. If it does work, let me say farewell in advance and tell you I shall miss your company."

Lionel gazed at the frail wishbone. He hesitated, then replaced it in the leather pouch.

"What's this, what's this?" asked Dr. Tudbelly. "You can be home in a jiffy, and you'd rather tramp all the way to Dunstan Forest?"

"No," said Lionel. "I'm not going."

"Not going?" cried Dr. Tudbelly. "I never took you for a lad who'd break a promise."

"I mean, I'm not going right away. I'm going back to Brightford first."

Dr. Tudbelly jumped to his feet and began opening the Armamentarium. "You barely got out of Brightford with a whole skin. And now you want to turn around and go back? To Pursewig? To Swaggart? They'll give you a welcome! Straight into the lock-up! You've lost your wits! What have I here for brain fever? Water must have leaked into your cranium!"

"I want to help Gillian," Lionel insisted. "I should never have left her in the first place."

"Gillian would be the last person in the world to have you risk your neck." Dr. Tudbelly peered curiously at Lionel. "Furthermore, if you're the cat you claim, none of this is your concern."

"It is my concern, even so," Lionel answered. "It wasn't, at first. But now it is. I don't understand it myself. It feels so odd— No, I'll not go home until I'm sure Gillian's in no harm."

"Oho, so that's how it is," Dr. Tudbelly sighed. "Water in your cranium? No, Gillian on your mind. If you ask me, you've gone and fallen in love."

"Is that worse than falling into Brightford River?" asked Lionel.

"Much worse," Dr. Tudbelly replied. "Well, my boy, if you're determined, let's head for Brightford *ex post facto.*"

"You'll come back with me? After all you warned against?"

"Reluctantly," admitted Dr. Tudbelly, "and against my better judgment. But if a cat can be so bold—well, indeed, so can a *doctorus medicus.*"

Lionel shouldered the Armamentarium and, with the illustrious Tudbelly behind him, set off along the riverbank. Soon, however, the underbrush grew thick and impassable, forcing him to turn away from the river and seek an easier path.

While Lionel's only thought was to reach The Crowned Swan as fast as he could, Dr. Tudbelly scrutinized every clump of weeds and shrubbery. The illustrious doctor continually hitched up his flapping robe to go crashing through dry grass or briars, never missing a chance to garner some new specimen for his Armamentarium.

"You see, my boy," Dr. Tudbelly explained, as they

halted to rest, "your common, garden-variety herbalist only mashes up odds and ends of this and that. The result? *Nota bene*—not worth a bean! Oh, perhaps for treating blisters, quinsy, hiccups, ingrown toenails, ague, rheumatism, shortness of breath—the ordinary run of complaints."

"Poor creatures!" cried Lionel. "Do humans suffer from so many ailments?"

"That's not half of them. Nor the worst of them, sad to say. No, my boy, those are the simplest. It's easier to treat dandruff on a man's head than meanness in his heart. I have a splendid cure for bunions. If only I could find one for greediness; or cruelty; or even plain every-day nastiness. Until I do, we unhappy creatures will have to get along as best we can. And speaking of that, you and I had best be getting along. *Ad astra per aspera*—watch out for snakes."

They started off again, but Lionel soon halted once more. A while before, he had skirted the edge of a wood. Now, instead of having left it behind him, he had come back to what appeared to be the same stand of trees.

"I don't understand this," he murmured. "I was following the same direction as the river—no, the opposite direction, because we drifted downstream. Brightford must be straight ahead. Or—or is it the other way?"

He stared at Dr. Tudbelly. "I don't know where we are. I'm lost!"

CHAPTER XIII

A Wagon Ride
and a Barrel of Herring

§✦ "*Non compos mentis*—I haven't the least idea," Dr. Tudbelly said. "I leave these matters entirely up to you."

"But I'm lost!" Lionel blurted. "A cat, lost! That's the first time it's ever happened. What's wrong? Am I sick?"

Dr. Tudbelly eyed the distraught Lionel. "What are your symptoms? Do you feel baffled? Bewildered? Confused? A little edgy? Frightened? Puzzled?"

"Yes, yes!" cried Lionel. "All of that!"

"Good," said Dr. Tudbelly. "You're quite normal."

"But what shall I do?"

"Why, the same as any sensible person in the circumstances. Keep going. Hope for the best. I don't know how it is with cats, but for a human it's the only way."

This advice gave Lionel no comfort, but he could do no more than follow it. Choking back his distress, he plucked up as much heart as he could and started off again. At last, when his hopes had begun to sink, he gave a glad cry. Ahead lay a wide and well-paved road. He ran to it, then halted, frowning:

"Brightford Road? It must be. But which way to town?"

"A difficult question," said Dr. Tudbelly. "The only good thing about it is that you have as much chance of being right as you have of being wrong."

At that moment, Lionel heard the clop of a horse's hoofs and the rattle of wheels. A cart lumbered into sight, and he waved his arms urgently at the driver:

"Friend, which way to Brightford?"

"Since that's where I'm going," retorted the driver, a bald-pated, high-shouldered man, skinny as a string, "I'd say it was in the direction my horse is pointed."

"Let us ride with you," Lionel pleaded. "We have to get there as fast as we can."

"My dear sir," Dr. Tudbelly put in, "you must realize your stroke of good fortune. In recompense for your kindness, I shall prepare you a poultice of *Tonsoria Tudbellia*, better known as Tudbelly's Hair Invigorator."

"Rub it on your own head," the driver flung back. "There's no room in my wagon for idlers and rogues, and I can tell at a glance that's what you are. If you weren't, you'd have your own wagon and not impose on a busy man's good nature."

At that, he clicked his tongue, slapped the reins, and set off with the wagon so quickly that Lionel had to dance out of the way to keep his toes from being run over.

"*Persona non grata!*" muttered Dr. Tudbelly. "Ungrateful fellow!"

"What sort of man is that?" Lionel cried bitterly, staring after the wagon. "He had room for a dozen! And insulting us, into the bargain! Swaggart would have taken wagon and all, if he were in my place. And that's what I should have done!"

"Stealing his wagon would hardly encourage him to be any more generous," Dr. Tudbelly said. "And if you did behave like Swaggart, you might wonder how much difference there was between you."

Lionel did not answer, but trudged along glumly, satisfied at least to know in which direction Brightford lay. Soon after, when he heard the rumble of another cart coming down the road in the opposite direction, he did not trouble to raise his head until the vehicle halted and a voice called:

"What, the two of you again? Swaggart's hunting you. If you keep on, you'll walk right into his hands."

It was Master Tolliver. Lionel hurried to the cart, glad to see a friendly face after a sour one.

"Go back to town?" exclaimed Tolliver, after Lionel told him what had happened. "Now? Of all times? Swaggart has a close watch on the inn. Gillian might as well be a prisoner in her own house."

"All the more reason for me to be with her," said Lionel. To his astonishment then, he saw Master Tolliver back up the wagon and turn it around.

"If you put it that way," Tolliver declared, "all the

more reason for me to lend a hand. Jump in, both of you. Climb under the canvas. Don't mind those barrels of herring. There's room for all of you."

Still amazed at Tolliver's unasked for and unexpected aid, Lionel helped Dr. Tudbelly into the back of the wagon, then climbed up beside the illustrious doctor. With the Armamentarium between them, the two crouched amid the wooden casks.

The wagon rattled along at a good pace, and soon clattered over Brightford Bridge, past the toll gate where Lionel heard a guard's voice:

"You again, Tolliver?"

"Some business left undone. It slipped my mind. Now I have to go back. Come on, be a good fellow. Forget the toll this time and let me pass."

Lionel heard the guard's curt refusal and Tolliver's loud grumbling as he paid the toll. The wagon rumbled over the cobbles of the market place. From what little he could see between the slats, Lionel judged the wagon was rapidly approaching the inn. Soon he glimpsed The Crowned Swan. As Tolliver had warned, a Watchman loitered by the doorway.

"I thought we'd seen the last of you," said the guard, as Tolliver reined up. "Move on. Or this time you'll have more trouble than you bargained for."

"I won't be cheated of my due," replied Tolliver, making a show of indignation. "I was promised payment for meat and flour. I won't be put off any longer."

"Go ahead, then," said the Watchman, after thinking

over the matter. "The wench is quick with a broom; but that's your risk, not mine."

"So it is," Tolliver declared, "and I'd rather not settle my business in the street."

The Watchman stepped aside and allowed Master Tolliver to turn horse and wagon into the inn yard, where he halted and rapped loudly at the back door. Owlbert cautiously peered out and Tolliver whispered hastily in his ear. The potboy disappeared and in another moment returned with Gillian, who ran to the wagon.

"I thought you were safe," the girl cried through the slats to Lionel. "What foolish thing have you done?"

"I was hoping you'd be pleased to see me," said Lionel. "Dr. Tudbelly thinks I've fallen in love. For that, I can't say, because it's never happened to me before. Even so, I'm not going home until all goes well with you."

Gillian flushed, laughing and crying at the same time. "Even a cat would have better sense! What good for either of us if you're caught? You're in worse danger than ever! And so am I."

"Then come to Dunstan Forest with me," Lionel urged. "Nothing can harm us there."

"And let Pursewig have the inn? He'd like nothing better!"

"Let him," returned Lionel. "It's only a house."

"No!" Gillian cried. "Pursewig takes all he wants in Brightford. Someone has to put a stop to it. If I don't stand up against him, none of us can call our lives our own."

Before Lionel could answer, Master Tolliver stepped to the wagon and raised his voice as if quarreling with Gillian. Lionel soon understood the reason. From his cramped hiding place, he glimpsed the Town Watchman and heard the man declare to someone:

"And I swear I saw her talking and whispering away to a barrel of herrings."

"Talking to herrings? The wench has lost her wits. Or you've lost yours," snapped the other voice, which Lionel recognized as Swaggart's.

Lionel crouched in the wagon. Swaggart strode up to Gillian:

"Now, mistress, my man says you were gossiping with herrings." He laughed roughly. "Tell me, did the herrings answer?"

"I'd rather talk to a kipper than to you," Gillian flung back. "Be off, rubbish, or I'll sweep you out again."

"Change your recipe, mistress," replied Swaggart. "More sugar and not so much sauce. You'd have less trouble if you and I were fonder friends."

Grinning, Swaggart reached out to take Gillian by the waist. Seeing this, Lionel, roaring furiously, threw aside the canvas, seized a barrel, and heaved it at Swaggart's head. The cask, however, missed its mark and only glanced off Swaggart's shoulder, to split open and shower him with herrings.

"*Ignis fatuus!*" cried Dr. Tudbelly, popping up from his hiding place. "The fat's in the fire now!"

Master Tolliver sprang forward. Owlbert burst

through the door, leaped on the Watchman's back, and gripped the astonished fellow's ears as if they were reins.

Lionel, that same instant, launched himself in a powerful spring. He leaped from the wagon, hands outstretched to grapple with Swaggart. But next thing Lionel knew, he was tumbling head over heels. For the first time in his life, he had failed to land on his feet. And now he sprawled helpless in Swaggart's clutches.

CHAPTER XIV

Mayor Pursewig Tries a Case

❧ Gillian ran to help Lionel. Throwing herself on Swaggart, she pounded her fists against his head and shoulders. Owlbert clung to his opponent's back, kicking sharply against the captain's ribs. Master Tolliver had collared two Town Watchmen at once, and was shaking both of them with all the strength of his burly arms. Dr. Tudbelly struck out with fists and feet in every direction. For a moment, the tide of battle turned. Under Gillian's pummeling, Swaggart at last fell back and Lionel scrambled free.

"Away with you!" Tolliver shouted, gripping a Watchman's head under each arm. "Take my wagon!"

Dr. Tudbelly, willing to beat a retreat, began clambering into Tolliver's cart. Lionel, however, refused to mount. In spite of Gillian's urging, he planted himself beside the girl, ready to face Swaggart again.

By now, more Watchmen had raced into the inn yard. Swaggart thrust his face at Gillian:

"Vixen! You'll wish you'd sung me a sweeter tune! And you, Puss! You and I have an old score to settle." He gestured to the officers, who closed ranks around their prisoners. "Take them away, all of them."

"My Armamentarium!" cried Dr. Tudbelly.

"Your box of rubbish, you mean," retorted Swaggart. He hauled the chest from the wagon and beckoned to one of the Watchmen. "Here, get rid of this."

Dr. Tudbelly flung his arms around the wooden case. Swaggart tried to pull it away, but Gillian struck his hands aside.

"You've no right to harm us or anything that belongs to us," she declared. "We've done no crime and we've been accused of none."

"Oho," crowed Swaggart, with a mocking bow. "Hear the learned judge."

"She's right, Swaggart," called one of the townsmen drawn by the commotion to the inn yard.

"You stay out of this," Swaggart flung back. "The law's my business, not yours." However, aware of angry mutterings from the townsfolk, he grudgingly allowed Dr. Tudbelly to keep hold of the Armamentarium.

At Swaggart's order, the officers marched their prisoners out of the yard and into the street. Gillian strode, head high, with Owlbert trotting at her heels. Dr. Tudbelly followed, while Master Tolliver kept a firm pace beside Lionel, who said glumly to him:

"You'd have been better off if you hadn't tried to do us a good turn."

"I suppose I would," replied Tolliver, with a grin. "Even so, I'd do the same again."

Lionel looked at him in surprise. "Why, not even a cat would make the same mistake twice."

"Well, now," said Tolliver, "what may be true for a cat isn't always true for a man. I might regret doing a wrong thing, but I'll surely never be sorry for doing a right thing. Tell me this: Would you have done any differently?"

Lionel blinked, puzzled a moment. "I—indeed, I'd do the same, come to think of it."

The prisoners were now herded into the stone building and room which Lionel remembered from his first day in Brightford. There, the officers prodded them into a corner and stood with pikes at the ready.

"This is no proper court," Gillian cried angrily. "Take us to the Town Hall. The Council must hear any charge against us."

"And so they will," declared a shrill voice that Lionel recognized immediately.

In the doorway stood Pursewig, red-robed, his chain of office around his neck. His little eyes gleamed, he rubbed his hands, and his knuckles crackled sharp and dry as his voice:

"The Council, unfortunately, is busy at the moment, about to pass my proposal to raise the tax on windowpanes. They cannot be disturbed. They shall, however, be given a full report. Master Swaggart, note down their statements."

Pursewig seated himself behind the wooden table. Beside him, Swaggart tilted his plumed hat to the back of his head, opened a crusted inkpot, gripped a quill pen, and began laboriously scribbling away.

"Is he noting down our statements?" Lionel asked. "So far, we haven't made any."

"Silence!" cried Pursewig. "I'll deal with you soon enough." He glanced at Master Tolliver. "Now, then: What's this one guilty of?"

"Aiding two criminals to escape from Brightford," announced Swaggart.

"They've not been judged criminals," Gillian burst out.

"They will be," Pursewig assured her. "And you along with them."

"*Reductio ad absurdum*—utterly ridiculous!" put in Dr. Tudbelly. "We weren't escaping. We were going back into town as fast as we could."

"That's right," added Tolliver. "I should know, since I was the one who took them into Brightford."

Pursewig frowned and muttered to Swaggart, "Don't you have a better charge than that?"

Swaggart, chewing the end of his quill, thought for a moment, scribbled on his blotted page again, then quickly added:

"Yes, Your Honor. A very serious one. Grievous assault by means of a barrel of herrings."

"I threw the barrel," cried Lionel, "not Master Tolliver."

"They were his herrings, nonetheless," Pursewig

77

snapped. "Herrings used as a deadly weapon. Very well. Confiscate them. Impound them in my larder, that's the safest place for such evidence."

Ignoring Tolliver's angry protest, Pursewig turned his attention to Owlbert. "And this villain, what's he done?"

"A notorious associate of the accused," replied Swaggart.

"Accused?" cried Gillian. "Accused of what? You have nothing against him or any of us."

"Impeding justice, for one thing," said Swaggart. "For another, abusing and ill-treating officers of the law, along with this other scoundrel, this charlatan—"

"*Doctorus medicus!*" Dr. Tudbelly burst out. "Charlatan, indeed! Sir, you insult my professional capacity."

"Hold your tongue," ordered Pursewig. "The court knows a charlatan when it sees one."

"He was last observed in company with another arch-rogue and public nuisance," continued Swaggart.

"If you mean me," said Lionel, "you have it wrong way round. I was helping Gillian. You were the nuisance."

"Silence!" cried Pursewig, rapping on the table. "I'll judge the facts for myself."

"They're already noted down," said Swaggart. "And the verdict. Guilty as charged."

"Guilty?" exclaimed Lionel. "Of what?"

"That will be determined in due course," replied Pursewig. "One thing sure: You're guilty of something. Otherwise, you'd not be on trial in the first place. To begin with, you filled my house with rats."

"Your Honor, they went of their own accord."

"How dare you say that! No rat would choose to live in my house!"

"Likely not," agreed Lionel, reconsidering. "I suppose they couldn't find a better place."

"What?" sputtered Pursewig. "You imply my residence isn't good enough for rats?"

"On the contrary, Your Honor, I'm sure it is."

"Enough!" shouted Pursewig. "You'll not bandy words with me! You've plotted with my enemies! Confess it! I'll have the truth! A pair of thumbscrews will squeeze it out of you! Swaggart, do your duty!"

CHAPTER XV

Disorder in Court

⊱ Before Swaggart could lay hands on the prisoners, the door of the guard room opened and Master Fuller, followed by the rest of the Town Council, strode to Pursewig's table. Swaggart, snarling, turned away.

"Your Honor," said Fuller in a stern voice, "we have heard that a trial is to be held."

"Wrong, Councilman," declared Pursewig. "It has just been held."

Master Fuller shook his head. "This is highly irregular. Your Honor, as you well know, the Town Charter requires the presence of all the Council if the case is a serious one."

"You waste your time," said Pursewig. "This is none of your concern. A matter of no consequence."

"I don't know what the other consequences are," put in Lionel, "but one of them is a pair of thumbscrews."

"Torture?" exclaimed Fuller. "This, too, is against the Town Charter. Mayor Pursewig, the Council will not condone your conduct of this trial."

"How dare you!" retorted Pursewig. "You question my authority?"

"Yes, when you go beyond it," replied Fuller, looking severely at the Mayor, while the other Council members murmured their approval.

"Masters, masters!" cried Pursewig, alarmed at seeing the Council side with Fuller. Gentling his tone, he raised his hands innocently. "You're quite mistaken. I'm doing no more than my duty. A humble public servant—"

"Public servant?" Gillian called out. "He's serving himself better than anyone. He wants my inn, there's no secret about that. If he can pack us off to prison, he'll take The Crowned Swan for himself."

"Mistress Gillian brings a grave charge against you," said Fuller. "The Council must hear both sides of this affair. Meantime, unless you can prove your accusations, you have no right to keep her prisoner."

Pursewig did not answer immediately, but grimaced and puffed out his cheeks. Swaggart stepped close to him and whispered hurriedly in his ear. Pursewig listened carefully and a smile trickled slowly over his face as he said:

"You are quite correct, Master Fuller. My Chief Constable points out the—ah, the intricacies of the case. Master Tolliver shall keep his herrings. All charges against him are dismissed. He is free to go. Mistress Gillian and the potboy shall have a full hearing tomorrow, in the presence of the entire Council. However, since she is a defendant, she is required to remain at The Crowned Swan until summoned to court. As for the two other defendants, they are to be held in custody until the trial resumes."

"You've no cause to hold them," Gillian cried.

"Silence!" ordered Pursewig. "They are not citizens of Brightford. Therefore, they can be detained as I direct. Furthermore, they must answer another complaint. Swaggart and his officers will testify. These two, knowingly, willingly, and with malice aforethought, removed their corporeal presence from an interriparian structure for the purpose of absconding without disbursement of a legally constituted financial obligation."

"What he says," Dr. Tudbelly muttered to the puzzled Lionel, "is that we crossed Brightford Bridge without paying any toll."

"But we didn't cross the bridge," Lionel protested. "We jumped off. And the reason we jumped off is that we were being shot at with those things called crossbows. We'd have been fools to stand there. Those Watchmen were actually trying to hurt us! As for paying a toll, the bridge belongs to my master. Magister Stephanus is the one who built it in the first place."

The guard room fell silent. Pursewig's jaw dropped and his face went livid. Master Fuller was the first to speak, and he went to Lionel, saying in a low voice:

"What are you telling us, young man? Have a care, this is a serious accusation."

"Is that what you call it?" returned Lionel. "It's only what Magister Stephanus himself told me. Years ago, when he was in Brightford, a man asked him to build a bridge for the good of all the town. And so he did. But after he finished, that fellow took it for his own and made everyone pay to go across it."

"Are you saying, then," Master Fuller went on, looking closely at Lionel, "that the Pursewigs were not the rightful owners? That they had no claim to it?"

"Liar! Liar!" shouted Pursewig, clenching his fists. "The bridge is mine, handed down from one Pursewig to the next! The toll gate, mine! I claim every right!"

Master Fuller raised a hand. "No doubt you do. But the justice of your claim is a different matter, and must be examined carefully. Your toll gate has been a heavy burden on our townsfolk. If the bridge was meant for the good of all, this young man has done Brightford the greatest service by telling us about it."

"What?" sputtered Pursewig. "You'll take a criminal's word against your own Mayor's?"

Master Fuller turned to Lionel. "Can you prove what you have told us?"

Lionel shook his head. "No."

"There you are!" squealed Pursewig. "A pack of lies! He admits it! He can prove nothing! Swaggart, take him away!"

"I can't prove it," Lionel continued, "but there's one who can: Magister Stephanus."

"Excellent!" cried Pursewig, gleefully clapping his hands. "Splendid! Let's hear from him. Built the bridge, did he? Then he must be as old as my great-grandfather, and just as long in his grave!"

"No, Your Honor," said Lionel. "He's not in any grave at all. He's in a cottage in Dunstan Forest."

"Will he come to Brightford?" Master Fuller asked. "Will he testify on your behalf?"

"I'm sure he won't," Lionel answered frankly. "He's vowed never to set foot in Brightford again. From what I've seen for myself, I can't say I blame him."

Master Fuller frowned. "Then perhaps we can go there?"

"I don't know," said Lionel. "He's not fond of company. But I could show you the way to his cottage."

"Trickery! Trumpery!" Pursewig broke in. "I'll not accept it! This villain's master will be just as great a liar. Enough! Court's adjourned!"

"The Council will not let these questions go unanswered," said Master Fuller. "We have overlooked your conduct in the past. But no longer. Mistress Gillian and this young stranger have set a brave example for us. We shall take up the proceedings again tomorrow."

"Adjourn! Adjourn!" shouted Pursewig. "Clear the court!"

Though Lionel fought to reach Gillian's side, Swaggart's officers surrounded him and Dr. Tudbelly and dragged them out of the guard room.

"Be calm, my boy," Dr. Tudbelly urged, clutching the Armamentarium as the guards hustled them along a narrow corridor. "Master Fuller will get to the root of it. You did splendidly. Pursewig should be worried, not you. Gillian's safe; and the worst that can happen to us is a night in the lockup."

Lionel took some comfort from the illustrious doctor's assurance. His heart sank, nevertheless, when he saw the open door of the cell. He turned to Swaggart, who was grinning crookedly at him.

"Laugh now, if you want," Lionel cried. "By tomorrow, you and your master—"

"Fool!" Swaggart broke in. "Do you think I mean to let you live that long?"

CHAPTER XVI

Dr. Tudbelly's Last Recipe

☙ The heavy door clanged shut. Lionel flung himself against it, beating at the iron plates, raging at Swaggart and Pursewig. Then, worn out by these useless efforts, he fell to his knees and covered his face with his hands. A moment later, he cried:

"Dr. Tudbelly! Help me! Something terrible is happening!" He licked at the salty droplets pouring down his cheeks. "My eyes! My eyes are leaking!"

Dr. Tudbelly smiled sadly and put a hand on Lionel's shoulder. "No harm. It's perfectly natural. *Hinc illae lacrimae*. We call them 'tears.'"

Lionel snuffled and rubbed curiously at the moisture from his eyes. "Do they come out often?"

"Not from cats," Dr. Tudbelly replied. "Among humans, alas, all too frequently. But, my boy, you've no cause to weep."

"Haven't I?" Lionel burst out. "I may never see Gillian again. We did no wrong. But we're caged up, Swaggart and Pursewig are free. Those villains put us here—and mean to kill us!"

"I don't know how things go in the world of cats," Dr. Tudbelly said, "but in the world of men, injustice isn't altogether *incognito*. But you have a key in your hands. That is, hanging round your neck. If your wishbone does all you claim."

Lionel's heart leaped as he clutched the leather pouch. He had forgotten the wishbone. Now he fumbled at the knotted drawstrings. He would be free of the stifling cell, and Brightford far behind him. Then he stopped.

"No. It can save only one of us. Take it. Wish yourself away. If you hadn't tried to look after me, you wouldn't be here now."

"My boy, I stayed with you because I chose to. I have no intention of leaving you now, of all times. One thing you should know about tears: They're utterly useless. No point in weeping. *Necessitas inventrix!* We need to get busy and do something."

"But we can't open the door, and that's the only way out," Lionel began. He glanced around the cell. "No—there's an opening of some kind, high up in the wall."

"Your eyesight's better than mine in the dark," Dr. Tudbelly said. "A grating? Barred? Can we pull it loose?"

Lionel sprang to the opening, struggled with the iron bars, and at last dropped back to the ground. "No chance. It won't budge."

"It will, my boy! It will! Yes, I should have thought

of it immediately!" The illustrious doctor began opening
the drawers of the Armamentarium. "*Solventia Univer-
salia Tudbellia:* Tudbelly's Universal Solvent."

"A potion for getting out of prison?" asked Lionel. "Do
we drink it? Or rub it on our heads?"

"No, indeed! We put it on the bars and melt them.
Tudbelly's Universal Solvent dissolves anything and
everything."

"Are you sure? Have you made it before?"

"Of course not. The one small difficulty with something that dissolves everything else is: What do you keep
it in? But I'll brew it in one of my beakers; we'll have a
moment or two before the beaker melts, long enough to
splash it on the bars. Then, out we go!"

Hurriedly, the illustrious doctor set about choosing
his ingredients. Then his face fell. "I forgot. The mixture
must boil. It needs a hot fire."

Lionel groaned. "No hope for us, then. There's nothing here to burn."

"I'm afraid you're right," Dr. Tudbelly glumly agreed.
Then he snapped his fingers. "Wait! We have all we
need. The Armamentarium! Smash it up! The thing will
blaze like tinder!"

"Burn the Armamentarium?" cried Lionel. "No, you
mustn't. It's priceless."

"You'd have given me your wishbone, wouldn't you?"
replied Dr. Tudbelly.

Heedless of Lionel's protests, the illustrious Tudbelly
filled a beaker with ingredients. He then emptied the

rest of the Armamentarium and threw the conglomeration of powders, roots, and dried leaves into a corner. For a long moment, he gazed fondly at the wooden chest. He shut his eyes tightly, hopped into the air, and landed with all his weight on the cabinet. The Armamentarium shattered like matchwood.

Lionel heaped the broken bits into a pile. Drawing flint and steel from his robe, Dr. Tudbelly struck a spark. Within moments, a fire was blazing.

"It's bubbling!" Dr. Tudbelly exclaimed, peering at the beaker he had set amid the flames. "Splendid! Now, jump up to the grating again."

Lionel sprang to the bars and hung there by one hand while Dr. Tudbelly, having wrapped the container in cloth torn from his robe, stood on tiptoe to pass the concoction to Lionel.

"Pour it on, my boy! Hurry!"

Lionel tipped the steaming beaker over the bars. Then he stared and called down:

"I can't!"

"There's nothing easier! Just splash it on!"

"I can't," repeated Lionel. "I mean, *it* can't. It won't pour. It's stuck!"

To prove his words, Lionel upended the container and shook it. The liquid had turned solid.

Below, Dr. Tudbelly clapped his hands to his head, groaning:

"Backwards! I got the recipe backwards! Universal Solvent? No, the very opposite! A Universal Fixative!"

Dr. Tudbelly's Universal Fixative, Lionel realized, was apparently also a Universal Heater. Instead of cooling, the concoction grew hotter by the moment. With a hiss of pain, he flung away the beaker which now had turned red hot.

The container landed amid the pile of ingredients in the corner of the cell. Instantly, there came a burst of white flame and an earsplitting roar louder than a thunderclap.

Torn from the grating, Lionel hurtled through the air and was dashed to the ground, where he went rolling and sprawling on top of Dr. Tudbelly.

Head whirling, ears ringing, coughing and choking in the bitter-smelling cloud of smoke, Lionel staggered to his feet and lifted the illustrious doctor, who was staring, unblinking, straight ahead.

"Are you hurt?" cried Lionel. "What happened? Can you hear me?"

Dr. Tudbelly smiled dreamily. "Marvelous! Magnificent! *Pulveria Tudbellia:* Tudbelly's Instant Pulverizer."

"Whatever it is," exclaimed Lionel, "we're free!"

He seized Dr. Tudbelly's arm and pointed at the corner. In the stone wall there was now a large, jagged hole.

That same instant, with a rattling of bars and bolts, the iron door was flung open. Swaggart burst into the cell.

CHAPTER XVII

Water and Fire

❧ As the Watchmen crowded behind him, Swaggart raised his lantern. He gaped at the breach in the wall. Then, with a curse, he lunged forward.

Dr. Tudbelly, stunned by the explosion, was even more stunned by his own part in it; and he stood there so lost in wonder that Lionel had to take him by the scruff of the neck and push him through the hole, plunging after him into the open street.

Behind them, Swaggart and his men scrambled over the rubble. With another push from Lionel, the illustrious doctor took to his heels. Lionel followed, but lost his footing on the cobbles and lurched against the side of a building. In horror, he realized he was nearly blind.

Darkness had always been clear as day to him. Now he could make out only vague shapes and looming shadows. His cat's vision was gone. He flung up his hands as he pitched into a wall. The Watchmen were upon him.

In an instant, the half-blind Lionel was thrown to the

cobbles, bound and gagged. A stout canvas sack was pulled over his head and shoulders. Struggle though he did, Lionel was soon trussed up inside it. He heard Swaggart laugh harshly:

"Well, Puss, you've come to the end of your nine lives!"

Lionel next felt himself hoisted into a cart or wheelbarrow, jolted over the cobblestones in what direction he could not guess. After a time, the sharp rattling gave way to the crunch of gravel, then to a muffled sound which Lionel supposed to be turf. The vehicle stopped. Lionel was hauled out and dragged across the ground.

"Swaggart," muttered one of the Watchmen, "I don't much like this night's business. Give him a good beating, instead. Or lock him up till Pursewig settles that other matter."

"Get out, if you're too chickenhearted," snarled Swaggart. "Be off, you cowards! I'll deal with him myself."

Though stifling in the sack, Lionel had never left off struggling. At last he loosened the ropes holding his arms and pushed the gag from his mouth. Too late. A heavy boot drove against his ribs and he heard Swaggart growl:

"That should keep him quiet till I've done with him."

The bewildered Lionel now felt himself swung into the air; then a sudden, violent plunge downward, with a heavy weight pulling at his legs. Next instant, he gasped for breath as water closed over his head. He was drowning.

Lungs bursting, heart pounding, Lionel fought to

tear himself free of the sack, which only clung more closely to his nose and mouth. Down he spun, choking on the icy water that poured in upon him.

The wishbone!

With all his might, he twisted back and forth. The wet sack was a skin that gripped him as tightly as his bonds. Writhing and straining, he raised his hands to his throat and clawed at the leather pouch. For that moment, he longed for nothing more in all the world than the cottage in Dunstan Forest; to see Magister Stephanus quietly weeding the garden; to lap a bowl of warm milk. The pouch ripped open. The wishbone was in his fingers. He snapped it in two. With his last, failing breath he cried out:

"I wish—I wish to be with Gillian!"

In a sudden burst of light, he went whirling and tumbling dizzily, to stop with a bone-cracking jolt. His eyes blinked open. He sat up and stared openmouthed in horror. He was in The Crowned Swan. Beside him, outstretched and motionless, lay Gillian. Instead of water, he was drowning in flames.

The whole inn room blazed. He jumped to his feet, snatched up Gillian in his arms, and cast about desperately for a path of escape. An impassable sheet of fire covered one side of the room; a cloud of smoke hid the rest. Above the roar and crackle, he heard voices outside shouting for buckets of water. A window shattered as a townsman bravely strove to force his way inside, but a burst of flame drove him back again.

Fighting his own terror, choking back the panic of any animal surrounded by dreaded fire, Lionel staggered from the inn room to the kitchen. There, Owlbert sprawled on the floor.

Coughing, eyes smarting, Lionel set Gillian down beside the boy, and struggled with the door latch. Then, with shock, he realized the door was barred from the outside. Gillian and Owlbert had been deliberately locked in. Lionel kicked with all his strength against the wooden panels. At last, they splintered. The sudden rush of air fanned the flames around him. He stumbled back to Gillian, carried her, still unconscious, into the inn yard, then returned and hauled Owlbert to safety.

"Ah, there you are!" called Dr. Tudbelly, pushing past the onlookers. "Safe and sound, all of you? If only I'd found you sooner! That explosion somewhat addled my wits. I must have been wandering all over town. Whatever has happened?"

Lionel had no time to answer the illustrious doctor. From within The Crowned Swan came faint but desperate cries. Still another victim had been trapped there. Lionel plunged once again into the flames. The cries, louder and more frantic, came from the cellar.

Lionel threw open the door. A hot blast sent him reeling. He flung up his arms to shield his face, and dashed through the rain of sparks, down the blazing steps. At the bottom, caught between two fallen barrels, wriggling helplessly as flames shot up around him, lay Mayor Pursewig.

"Save me! Save me!" shrieked Pursewig as soon as he glimpsed Lionel. "I meant no harm. I only wanted a little fire—only a little one!"

"You?" Lionel burst out. "You did this?"

"Swaggart's idea!" bawled Pursewig. "Damage the inn, enough so the wench couldn't afford to repair it. Then she'd have to sell it to me!"

"Did you think of what might happen to Gillian?" cried Lionel. "You should roast in your own fire!"

"No! No!" screamed Pursewig. "I'll give you whatever you ask. My gold! All of it! My house! Everything!"

"They're no use to me," retorted Lionel. "But, to Gillian—"

"Gillian can have it all, then!" cried Pursewig. "I'll rebuild the inn for her! I'll work in her kitchen! I'll send Swaggart away! Replace his Watchmen! I'll take down the toll gate! I'll resign! Fuller can be Mayor! Only save me! My life! That's all I ask!"

As Pursewig yelled his pleas and promises over and over again, Lionel sprang down the flaming steps and wrestled away the heavy barrels. Pursewig, still shrieking for his life, rolled clear. Seizing him by the gold chain around his neck, Lionel hauled him from the cellar. Behind them, the stairs collapsed and the floor gave way. Dragging the Mayor with him, Lionel staggered to the safety of the inn yard. Gillian, regaining her feet, ran to throw her arms around Lionel.

"Stop!" commanded Pursewig. "You're all under arrest!"

CHAPTER XVIII

Mayor Pursewig's Promises

❧ "But—but you promised you'd rebuild the inn!" cried Lionel, holding Gillian closer. "And what about the toll gate? What about your gold?"

Grimy and disheveled, his robe still smoldering where sparks had burned holes in it, Pursewig folded his arms and snorted indignantly:

"I said nothing of the kind."

Dr. Tudbelly seized him by the collar with one hand and with the other shook a finger under his nose. "Indeed you did, sir! *Quod erat demonstratum*—what a show you put on! I heard every word."

"So did I," Gillian declared. "Give me my broom and I'll jog your memory!"

"I, too," called out Master Tolliver, shouldering his way through the crowd. "You were bawling your head off. We all heard you."

The townsfolk added their voices to Tolliver's, berating Pursewig so furiously that finally the Mayor grudgingly muttered:

"It slipped my mind. But if that's how you show your gratitude for all I've done for you—very well, so be it."

Owlbert, meanwhile, had pulled off his apron, which he now began tying around Pursewig's middle.

"Get away from me, you impudent pip-squeak," shouted the former Mayor. "What are you doing?"

"Why, Your Honor," said Owlbert, "it seems to me you mentioned something about working in the kitchen. No better time to start."

"Ridiculous!" Pursewig flung back. "A man of my capacities! Pots and pans? Beneath my notice!"

"Beneath your nose they'll be," said Owlbert. "Don't worry, I'll teach you what to do. I'll be your schoolmaster and we'll have lessons in scraping and scrubbing. You'll learn in no time. A sharp-witted fellow like you— why, you'll soon be the keenest, most joyful pot-scrubber in Brightford."

Still fuming, Pursewig followed his eager instructor through the inn yard. Dr. Tudbelly turned to Lionel and muttered:

"If you ask me, you should have let that wretch stew in his own juice."

"I couldn't," said Lionel. "I don't know why, but I couldn't leave him there to burn. Not him, not anyone."

"Not even Swaggart?" Dr. Tudbelly said. "Well, no matter. He's run off, and I daresay he won't show his face here again."

Gillian, throughout this, had been looking at Lionel with astonishment. "The last I remember was trying to put out the fire," she said. "No—the very last, I was wishing I could see you again. Next thing, there you were! I can't imagine how you managed to do it."

"My wishbone," said Lionel. "It brought me where I wanted most to be."

"Then it granted both our wishes."

Lionel sadly shook his head. "Alas, not all of mine. For now I'd wish we could stay together. But I promised Stephanus I'd come back to him, and so I must."

"I'm going with you, then," Gillian declared. "I'll have a few words with this master of yours. If you want to quit his service, he has no right to keep you like a prisoner. Of course, it's only fair to make sure he finds someone to fill your place; and do—well, whatever sort of work you did for him. Were you his apprentice? Truly, now. His gardener? His house servant?"

"His cat," insisted Lionel, despite Gillian's sigh of long-suffering patience. "But please come with me anyway, to say farewell before he changes me back again." He turned to Dr. Tudbelly. "Will you come with me, too? You lost your Armamentarium on my account. When I tell Magister Stephanus, he might give you some of his own herbs and potions to make up for it."

"Gladly, my boy," Dr. Tudbelly replied. "My mixture that blew such a hole in the wall—I should like to include it when I assemble a new and even better Armamentarium; for the life of me, though, I can't remember what went into it. I'll never be able to make it again. Perhaps your Magister Stephanus knows the recipe. There might be some occasional use for it. Digging out stumps, drilling wells. . . . No, on second thought, that compound's too noisy and messy. Hardly practical, and more trouble than it's worth."

"Then we'll all go to Dunstan Forest," Gillian agreed. "The journey and the fresh air should clear Lionel's head once and for all." She turned a fond glance to him. "And the sooner you recover, the better. Because," she added in a gentle tone, "once we're back in Brightford, I'll give you leave to court me."

"But we've already been to court—" Lionel began.

"This," replied Gillian, "is a different kind."

"Will I like it better than the other?"

Gillian smiled. "I think so."

That morning, Brightford was merry as if it had been a holiday and a dozen town fairs at once. Master Fuller, wearing the Mayor's gold chain around his neck, gave the first ax-blow to the toll gate. The townspeople wasted no time tearing down the rest of it. At The Crowned Swan, carpenters and masons had begun mending the damage, and the folk of Brightford gladly lent a hand. Master Tolliver had offered to carry the three travelers in his cart and set them well on their way. As the wagon rumbled through the town, Lionel, with Gillian and Dr. Tudbelly beside him, had a glimpse of Pursewig sitting in the inn yard, an enormous pot between his knees, scrubbing away vigorously under the watchful eye of Owlbert.

At the edge of Dunstan Forest, Lionel took grateful

leave of Master Tolliver. As the wagon disappeared around a bend in the road, Lionel beckoned for Gillian and Dr. Tudbelly to follow him.

"I remember this path," Lionel said. "At any rate, I think I do."

Taking Gillian's hand, he helped her through a gap in the brambles. Dr. Tudbelly puffed along behind, hanging back as usual to study whatever vegetation caught his interest. They had scarcely been long on their way, however, when the illustrious doctor raised a hand and called out in warning:

"*Habeas corpus!* I hear somebody in the bushes."

"We're safer here than we ever were in Brightford," Lionel began. Next instant, he shouted an alarm.

From behind a tree stepped Swaggart. His plumed hat was gone, his white ruff befouled, his uniform torn; but he grinned, cocked his head as arrogantly as ever, and raised the crossbow he carried.

"So, Puss, you've run off without a farewell to me? And taken the little vixen with you? But you've left our score unsettled."

"Be gone, Swaggart!" Gillian cried. "You've done harm enough. Pursewig can't help you now. Set foot in Brightford and it will be worth your skin."

"For that, I have your swain to thank," returned Swaggart, bringing his weapon to bear on Lionel.

"This gentleman is on his way to join his master," put in Dr. Tudbelly. "You'd be wise not to interfere."

"Let Puss run home, then," Swaggart flung back, "if he can run faster than this."

Before Lionel could move, Gillian flung herself against Swaggart and snatched at the crossbow. The bolt went hissing past Lionel's head. Swaggart fell back, twisted away, still clutching his weapon, and dashed through the underbrush.

Roaring, Lionel plunged after him, deeper into the forest, heedless of the briars that tore at him as he raced on, stumbling and slipping on moss-covered rocks, clambering over fallen trees. But, as he tried to leap a dry stream bed, he tripped and went pitching headlong.

Stunned for an instant, he sat up and shook his head to clear his wits. What had sent him sprawling was neither stone nor root, but Swaggart's crossbow lying abandoned on the ground, with a handful of bolts scattered beside it.

Lionel seized the weapon, ready to wind the bowstring taut. Then, with a cry, he smashed it against a boulder and flung away the shattered pieces.

He fell back to his knees and cried out again in astonishment. Magister Stephanus stood before him.

In Which Lionel Goes Home

੭ᯍ Magister Stephanus held a beanpole in one hand, a garden spade in the other. He looked sternly down at Lionel:

"Home at last, are you? I should say it was about time. You've kept your promise. That much, at least, I find commendable. Would you kindly inform me what you were going to do with that crossbow?"

"A man—Swaggart," Lionel began. He bowed his head. "I wanted—for a moment, I wanted to kill him."

"So it would appear." Stephanus frowned. "I'm glad you had better sense. I recall you were gentler as a cat than you seem to be as a man. Come. The cottage is nearby."

"But Gillian's life is in danger," Lionel protested. He pulled away as Magister Stephanus reached out to take his former cat by the arm. "And Dr. Tudbelly! I can't leave them in the woods. Not with Swaggart on the loose. Master, let me find them."

"Stop!" ordered Stephanus, putting his hands to his ears as Lionel began stammering a hasty account of all that had happened to him. "It was distressing enough, seeing you in a rage like an ordinary human. Now you're gabbling worse than any of them. This creature Swaggart will harm no one."

Just then, with Gillian beside him, Dr. Tudbelly emerged from a thicket. The illustrious doctor stopped short. At sight of Stephanus, Gillian, too, halted. The ancient wizard's glance and bearing made her lower her eyes, as she murmured:

"Lionel told me his master changed him from a cat into a man. I didn't believe him."

"And now you do?" replied Stephanus. "And so you should. I assure you it is quite true. Cat he was; cat he will be again."

Gillian hesitated a moment, then raised her head to look squarely at Stephanus. "Have you asked him if he wants to?"

The wizard's eyes flashed. "Of course not. Young woman, what he wants or doesn't want has nothing to do with the matter."

"How can you say that?" Gillian cried. "Because you have the power to work your will as you please? It means nothing, what a person wants to be? Or doesn't want to be?"

Stephanus made a wry face, taken aback at being so sharply questioned. "I feel no obligation to give an accounting to you or any human. But, to satisfy you: a person, you said? Very well. My cat is not a person. Furthermore, since he belongs to me—"

"Belongs?" Gillian exclaimed. "Do you think anyone can own another's life? Cat, man, or whatever?"

Stephanus did not answer. Instead, he scowled, glared, and grumbled into his beard. Lionel whispered to Gillian:

"Be careful. Last time he was angry, he changed me into a man. He's likely to change you into a cat."

"Let him!" Gillian tossed her head and declared to Stephanus:

"If Lionel must be a cat, I'll be one along with him!"

"And give up your own life?" Lionel burst out. "After all you've gained in Brightford? No, no, Gillian, I won't ask that of you."

"You didn't ask," Gillian replied. "I offered."

Stephanus looked at Gillian with grudging admiration. "You're a determined creature, I'll say that much for you. A noble impulse. I had almost forgotten. You mortals do have them occasionally. But you shall stay as you are. I should feel happier knowing there was a human like you in Brightford."

"What of Lionel's happiness?" Gillian cried. "What of mine?"

"Important, no doubt. To you. In time, you'll get used to doing without it. Enough. I have my beans to tie. Come," the wizard ordered Lionel, then added to Gillian, "And you. I shall permit you to take a last leave of each other."

Dr. Tudbelly, fascinated by the plants and wild flowers, stopped his explorations to hitch up his robe and trot after Lionel, saying:

"I detect an unmistakable skunkiferous aroma. We must have roused one of those fellows when we ran through the woods. Yes, there he is."

Dr. Tudbelly pointed to a small, furry creature glaring beady-eyed from the bushes. It bared its teeth furiously and stood on its hind legs, front paws upraised and shaking like tiny fists. At a gesture from the illustrious doctor, the animal took fright and darted off.

Lionel slowly followed Magister Stephanus through the yard into the cottage. Seeing the familiar room, the wooden stools and table, the cupboard, the churn, he gave a cry of recognition. Amid the scent of dried herbs hanging from the walls, and the soup kettle simmering in the fireplace, his heart quickened and he was almost eager to be a cat once more. Then grief caught at his throat as he turned, silently clasped hands with Dr. Tudbelly and embraced Gillian, holding her in his arms until Stephanus drew him gently aside.

Lionel shut his eyes and turned his face away. He felt the wizard's hand on his shoulder and he waited, hardly daring to breathe. His head reeled and he dropped to his knees. His eyelids fluttered open. Gillian and Dr. Tudbelly were staring at him. Magister Stephanus had taken a pace backward.

"My spell—" murmured the wizard, frowning— "my spell has failed."

Lionel blinked. His hands were still the hands of a man, not the paws of a cat. He ran his fingers over the smooth skin of his face. With a joyous cry, Gillian went to his side.

"Get up," Stephanus ordered Lionel. "Stand on your two legs. They're the only ones you'll ever have."

"Master!" Lionel exclaimed. "You let me stay a man!"

The wizard snorted. "Not by my choice, you can be sure. You're beyond my skill. I sent you to Brightford, a perfectly acceptable cat. And now? Spoiled! You've been too long among those creatures! You've done things no sensible animal would ever dream of doing. I should have known immediately. You must have packed yourself with just about every imaginable human feeling. Quite hopeless. No, you'll never be a cat again. You've been tainted with humanity!"

"Master, then what—?"

Stephanus shook his head. "There's little I can offer you. If you care to stay here, you may do so. Under one condition: I shall have to cast another spell on you. You'll have no more human thoughts. Indeed, you'll forget you ever were a man."

Lionel said nothing for a moment. At last he replied, "Some of what happened to me—yes, I'd gladly forget. But the rest—?" He turned to Gillian. "No, that I always want to remember."

"Are you sure?" Stephanus asked. "You'd be quite safe here. Nothing would ever trouble you. You'd have a calm and peaceful life, not a care in the world; which is more than any mortal can expect. You've seen enough of these humans to know what they're like."

"They're all you said," Lionel agreed. "And worse, some of them; but some far better than you told me. If I can't have the good without the bad, I'll take all together."

"Foolish," sighed the wizard. "As foolish as all the others."

"Forgive me for interrupting," said Dr. Tudbelly, "but surely you have a potion, an unguent, that would do away with all those deplorable qualities we suffer? If you make the recipe available to me, I should be happy to name it in your honor: *Electuarius Stephanus.*"

"There is no such thing, magic or otherwise," replied Stephanus. "If there were, don't you think I'd have used it ages ago? Whatever hope there may be for you unfortunate creatures, you shall have to find it in yourselves. Now be off, all of you. I don't care to have humans cluttering up my cottage."

Lionel embraced the wizard. "Farewell, master. And thank you again for changing me into a man."

"Give me no thanks," replied Stephanus. "I put you into human shape. You made yourself into a human being."

As Lionel went to the doorway, Dr. Tudbelly anxiously whispered in his ear:

"Don't growl, my boy. *Optimus terminus!* Everything's turned out splendidly for you."

"He isn't growling," said Gillian. "He's purring." She took Lionel's hand. "Come, let's go home."

Lloyd Alexander's numerous honors include a Newbery Medal for *The High King*, a Newbery Honor for *The Black Cauldron*—both part of the Prydain Chronicles—and National Book Awards for *The Marvelous Misadventures of Sebastian* and *Westmark*. His five Vesper Holly Adventures are also beloved.

Lloyd Alexander lives with his wife, Janine, and their cats in Drexel Hill, Pennsylvania.